Critical acclaim

'There are new voices in British crime fiction fighting to be heard. Scary new voices who plot the story of the criminal underclass as they nibble away at the fabric of society. One such voice is Mark Powell. And quite a voice he's got, as his first novel illustrates. And I know I said crime fiction, but *Snap* is much more than a genre novel' *Independent on Sunday*

'*Snap* plunges into depths and strives to illuminate the tensions of brotherly love, place and identity for the kind of man who takes pride in not expressing emotion. It is workmanlike despite its depths, and profound in spite of its action-packed narrative' *Big Issue*

'As an exploration of the shifting relationship between siblings, Mark Powell's debut is occasionally poignant'   *The List*

'Pitched somewhere between Guy Ritchie and *Zigger Zagger* in tone, this defiantly unrealistic, insanely over-stylised romp is compelling'   *The Times*

'A must-read for anyone with a few hours to kill'   *FHM*

'Lyrical, organic and brutal'   *Jockey Slut*

At the age of nineteen, Mark Powell dropped out of university and moved to New York where he immersed himself in gangland street culture, living in Manhattan and the South Bronx. After three years travelling in Europe, North Africa and the Middle East he returned to England, completed a law degree and joined the RAF, before leaving to pursue a writing career. *Snap*, his first novel, won the Curtis Brown Award. Mark currently combines writing with working as a teacher for excluded schoolchildren in Brent, north-west London.

SNAP

MARK POWELL

PHOENIX

A PHOENIX PAPERBACK

First published in Great Britain in 2001
by Weidenfeld & Nicolson
This paperback edition published in 2001
by Phoenix,
an imprint of Orion Books Ltd,
Orion House, 5 Upper Saint Martin's Lane,
London WC2H 9EA

A CIP catalogue record for this book
is available from the British Library.

ISBN 0 75381 300 9

Printed and bound in Great Britain by
Clays Ltd, St Ives plc

for HB

Acknowledgements

Stephanie Aldred, LTJ Bukem, the Curtis Brown agency, Anna Davis, Richard Francis, Sara Holloway, Christine Kidney, Greg Leach, Adrian Slatcher.

Falling Angels

1

It is spring. It is midnight; light rain dusts the high-rise window. In the shallow light of a lamp West sits at the table sorting matchsticks, using a knife to cut them into the required shapes.

It is quiet; even the music from his brother's room next door has stopped. West works well in the hush; only the sound of his strained breathing making a noise, barely noticed in his concentration.

He does not usually model after an evening in the pub, but tonight the sticks and glue appealed. The delicate work relaxes him and readies him for sleep.

Outside the room a door slams.

– You just don't give up, do you!

The shout belongs to Girl Garner, his brother's girlfriend.

Hurried steps along carpet. West lowers the blade and holds his breath to listen.

– Come back here, for fuck's sake. What's a matter with you, Gee Gee? West's brother calls from the other bedroom.

– You're a bastard, a bastard! the girl yells back along the corridor.

– Just take it easy and get your arse back in this room, you hear me?

No reply, just the urgent press of buttons on plastic.

West hears Gee Gee – Girl Garner – muttering into the telephone. He hears his brother push open the door.

– Oh, you're not really gonna phone him. Leave it.

West does not move. He just listens, as he so often does. Looking out of the window, seeing the vastness of inner-city lights from twelfth-floor eyes.

– If you're going to start all this business you're going to have to get your kit, babe, the brother shouts. The voice is unconvincing, swallowed by the silence. – What the fuck am I meant to have done?

Outside the window, the stench of rubber and refuse. Inside, the stench of dust and anger. The bulb in West's lamp appears to dim. He wants to turn it off. Sit in anonymity.

He can tell that East, his brother, has not left the bedroom doorway. He has not gone to Girl Garner, by the phone, to appease her. He is calling out, ignoring her sobs.

– If it's about you getting fat I don't get your fucking problem. It's a fact, it's not me.

West lifts himself from the chair, flicking the lamp off. Darkness, and he breathes normally again. Tiptoes over to the bed, lowers himself on to its comfort. With a brief cough and rustle of pillow he slips beneath the quilt. Back to listening.

Five, ten, minutes pass. The earlier events are absorbed by the night-time vacuum. West's eyes are open, alert, creating shapes and faces in the darkness, aware of unfinished business between his brother and Girl. The front-door latch clicks open, a controlled turn of the knob. He hears East run to the hall.

– Don't you dare go! What about your clothes?

The front door is slammed then wrenched open again. Noises resound in the building's corridor, by lifts, by concrete stairway. West gets out of bed and peers through his half-opened door. Sees nothing, though the front door is

open wide; hears vicious whispers and the panicked movements of feet and bodies. He makes his way quietly along the
hallway. The voices become clearer.

– Come back here, East growls.

– Piss off!

Urgent grunts, the clutch of flesh and pull of limb.

– Come here.

– Get off me!

Bodies collide and then a shriek, thumps, the clattering of
something falling.

– Gee Gee!

West runs into the outside corridor – no one there. To the
stairway. His naked brother is down a level, crouched by a
heap of hair and clothes. It is not a heap but Girl Garner.
West stares at his brother pulling and jerking at the body.

– Get up, Gee Gee. Get up. Don't mess about.

But she does not get up. She cannot get up. Her head is
twisted and blood seeps from her ears. Her torso is
misshapen, it lies slumped on concrete. Time stops as the
brothers stare at horror.

The lift doors part, Geezer Garner emerges, summoned on
phone and avenger of his sister's troubles. He is lit bright by
artificial light. Sees West and moves towards him.

– Where's your fucking brother?

West looks down as his brother looks up to the top of the
stairs. East does not register the presence of Geezer – who
suddenly stands frozen by the chill image below – but gropes
his stare towards his brother. West's face displays no
emotion. There is a serenity in West, a silent, immutable
loyalty. It is the face East needs.

– I think she's dead. I think she's fucking dead.

*

The hospital stands leviathan under a quarter-moon, rising out of sleeping shadows. Blue rays streak the waiting staff. Words like 'haemorrhage', 'spinal damage', and 'endotracheal' buzz through the long white avenues. Girl Garner is pushed on steel trolley over linoleum for an emergency scan. She is still alive; the heart pulsates, blood flows, yet corpse eyes stare nowhere. Machines operate with expensive groans, experts congregate to assess the extent of injuries to head, to spine. Not expecting to see a child.

– Oh my God, she's pregnant, the consultant declares.

Intensive care receives the patient – the patients. A ventilator pumps the lungs while senior staff perform tests and confirm suspicions; the brain of Girl Garner is dead, only the child genuinely lives. It is well developed, around thirty-two weeks, and remains curled peacefully, floating inside the female who is stabilised to secure its well-being. Decisions have to be made.

Geezer Garner waits by the reception nurse, who has a tight smile and blond hair wrapped under her hat. He has a mobile phone jammed into his mouth, barking to fellow members of the Garner clan.

Within an hour Geezer is joined by Father Garner, Mother Garner, Sister Garner and Bloke with his hair polished backwards in gel. They mill about in gold jewellery and leather jackets reeking of cigarettes, harassing white coats for information.

– That's my daughter in there. That's my bleedin' daughter!

– We are doing all we can, Mr Garner, I assure you.

Inflamed eyes, scarlet skin, rubbed red by nervous fingers, the family wait on plastic chairs, orange with black legs, surrounded by posters on walls (Is Your Child On Drugs?), and a dalek drinks machine. A vertical black tube topped with silver tray for ash and litter stands next to Father Garner, who pushes his face into hirsute hands. Mother Garner, silver-haired, holds Sister. Bloke scans the scene, noticing all, seeing nothing, wrestling with the sight on the tower-block staircase described by Geezer.

The doctor informs the Garners of the situation.

– No hope for her ... brain dead ... hope for the baby.

– Baby? What bleeding baby! Father Garner shouts. – Sod the baby, keep my daughter alive.

– Who's the father of the child? asks a doctor.

Geezer looks to Father, to Bloke, each set of eyes constrict as if exposed to bright light, each knows the details of Geezer's account.

– He's dead, Geezer says. – Dead.

The statement is followed by solemn nods from the clan standing in a circle about the white coat.

– Yeah, he's dead all right, adds Bloke, under his breath.

The next morning a decision has to be made. The baby has to be given the life that Girl Garner has lost. The lack of sleep on the plastic seats makes the Garner rage more volatile. Despite the threats, the experts agree unanimously that the child has to be pulled from the wreckage.

– Don't you take that bastard out of her, do you hear!

The police are called to restrain the family who launch heavy hands at doctors, nurses, those who condemned Girl to death.

The bright hygiene of theatre; so much brighter than the reluctant sun breaking from behind clouds outside. The scrubbed-clean hands of surgery; so much cleaner than the hands outside that grip bacon butties, steering wheels, coins in pocket for train, for bus, for journeys. And as the city yawns, opening itself up for another day, the scalpel of the surgeon slits open the flesh of Girl Garner.

It will be a daughter. A baby girl. Up for adoption.

Later on, in a soundless room, Geezer and Bloke stare at one another. They gaze vengeance. The life-support is turned off. Girl's lungs take their last toke of Tower Hamlets.

2

East knew she was dead as soon as he saw the heap enveloped by emergency tubes and drips, saw her lying on the stretcher and carried off into the harsh lighting of the corridor from which she fell. Geezer Garner strutted alongside the body, rearranging the blanket, glaring back. As Geezer entered the lift, last, he pointed straight at East. No words spoken, no expression, just a single poke of his finger. The ten-month relationship with Gee Gee had ended, ten months of drunken fights and drugged love. All that was left was the threat of that pointed finger.

But grief is not forthcoming, for East did not really love her. They shared roots, associates, lust, intoxication, but nothing that East would call love. And it was alcohol and amphetamine that final evening, following the usual rounds of insult, that had clinched fate, that sent her tumbling down the solid steps of the fire escape.

Now it is East who needs to escape, to get out of the flat. Things are happening too fast, he wants time to think.

The descent in the lift, so close to Girl Garner's departure, is eerie. Its metal walls are smeared with coloured words and sketches. Cables hum as the lift plunges from clouds to mud, yellow numbers flick from 7 to 6 to 5. The ground floor rumbles into view from behind wired glass, the door opens into gloom.

The tower block is one of three that burst from the earth; frozen geysers of cement and steel. Grass-clumped mud encircles the blocks; a wasteland moat, smothered with urban debris. There is a playground, full of metal frames and rusting swings where children fall, scream and meet to fight and spit away from adults.

At two in the morning even the yobs have fallen asleep in unkempt bedrooms without carpet or bedtime story, rolling about on mattresses under which weapons lie. The baggy-breeches, baseball-cap brigade are in bed. Their youthful domain, their muddy manor, rests from another day of battle. Yet there's no innocence as they shriek nightmares in high-storey homes.

The terrain is strangely serene. East wanders past dark railings – many ripped off as spears for the jungle – and drags his feet along the East End street. Parked cars nestle against the kerb, with occasional creaks of cooling metal. East walks alone. Alone with a pointing finger, fear of the Garner revenge.

West sits in the living room awaiting East's return. Death has hijacked their family before, forcing changes of direction. Tribute stands in gilt frame on the tiled mantelpiece above the gas fire: Mum and Dad at restaurant, clinking wine glasses, smiles stretching beyond the one-dimensional print. The smile of memory, in best clothes long gone.

Lenny – Dad – was Bow-born. He skipped school at fourteen to work with a mob who ran cargo between the markets: Spitalfields to Roman Road, Walthamstow and Romford. A lean, fit guy, a ladies' man who regarded a bit-on-the-side as harmless even when Sue – Mum – cried in the kitchen as she heard about the latest fling. She kept her unhappiness to herself, though – Lenny carried a temper beneath his extrovert personality, and the boys, too, found themselves at the sharp end. A hiding often awaited East if he forgot to drop off an errand, or pick up his brother from school. West had an easier time, being the youngest, and with his disease.

During holidays, the brothers would join Lenny on the back of the lorry, helping to unload sacks of potatoes, onions and carrots. Some days after work, when Lenny had dropped off his colleagues, he would drive the boys round to Aunty Pat's or Aunty Jean's. They would wait in the lounge with beakers of juice and the television while Dad 'popped upstairs to check the boiler'. They were not allowed to mention the stops to Mum. They never did; they knew the belt would be waiting.

Sometimes during the summer they would take the lorry down to Wapping and park up on the river-edge by the disused wharfs. The three of them would eat sandwiches bought from Percy Ingle and neck pints of milk, staring in silence along the river towards Tower Bridge, leaning against the truck, lapping up the sunshine.

Before they climbed back into the cab, Lenny and East would grab West and swing him over the edge of the wall, pretending to hurl him into the Thames. West thought this was hilarious.

The old man was killed by a police marksman following a West End jewellery job. The raid was rumbled. The response was to run. Dived into Regent Place, died in Regent Place, his skull detonated by a high-velocity round.

– This'll be the last one, I promise. Then I'm finished wiv this game, I'm out of it.

*

Mum was always on the boys' side. A beautiful woman with dark brown hair and deep eyes who did her best to satisfy Lenny and keep the boys happy. Cooked and cleaned, lied for her husband if he didn't want to be found, wrote excuse notes for her sons to take to school. Liked a drink and liked to hug West after the booze took effect. She would end up unconscious on the sofa at the end of the afternoon and the brothers would be sent down to the takeaway for tea. Sometimes Dad ignored her drunkenness, other times he would shout and push her around and then disappear for the night.

Sue rotted away from cancer soon after her husband was killed. Once they'd buried Dad she just fell to pieces. West took over the cooking and cleaning, East brought home chocolates, magazines and, occasionally, flowers. It didn't make any difference; she still moped around the flat and refused to change out of her dressing gown. The boys tried so hard to put her back together but she was busted up from the inside, in a place they could not reach.

And now Gee Gee was dead. West had noticed how East's face filled with awkwardness rather than grief as he looked up at him. As if she was an accident, a tea-spill on the carpet that had to be removed before visitors called. And a visitor had called. West saw the pointed finger, recoiled from its force as it retreated through graffiti doors.

The stares West normally received from strangers caused hurt but the glare from the lift terrified him, perhaps as much as his swollen face terrified the children who peered from behind adult legs. West had never got used to the attention that his condition had inflicted upon him: the abuse, the laughter, the prejudice. He hadn't acclimatised to the stifling heat of rejection, of being different, of wearing his ugliness like a crime.

His face blown up huge by neurofibromatosis, heaps of thick flesh spread over his head, West spent much of his childhood standing in front of the mirror pleading with the disease to leave him, to free him, only to observe the swelling grow and push his face behind a mask of mounded skin. His left eye shining blue, his right barely visible behind the flesh bulging from temple and forehead.

At the age of eighteen months the diagnosis was made from café-au-lait stains over his body that confirmed the illness; the prognosis was accurate. East, who also sported the coffee stains, was lucky. In him, the disease remained dormant. But West was transformed; the mutant gene took just one of the two.

His first six years were comparatively normal – the swelling was confined to a small area hidden under his hair. No one at home or school made much of the head bumps in the early years. This all changed when Darren Brazier identified the onset of bigger changes.

– What's that? he asked West, in the infants' playground, pointing to his cheek.

– What? West replied.

– That.

Darren took West to the toilets and showed him the lump pushing out from beneath his eye, like a bone trying to escape.

– I don't know what it is, West said.

The right side of his face had always felt harder than the left, but he had dismissed it until Darren noticed it growing outwards and pushing his eye closed.

Lenny and Sue did not trust doctors or dentists and West

was left to metamorphose. School teachers made home visits and insisted that social services were contacted, but the scene always turned nasty.

– You're not sending my son to one of those places! Sue screamed.

– But your son needs specialist help.

– My boy is not a mental.

And then Lenny would return from work and lose his temper and push the teachers out of the flat.

– You're the bleeding teachers, you bleeding well get on with teaching him.

– But he can hardly speak . . .

– You're not going to send my kid away! Got it?

Lenny and Sue's insistence prevailed, but they did not know what to do with their son. They hoped the problem would go away and made West lie in bed with a pack of ice over his face. One thing was for sure: they weren't going to allow others to get involved.

The growth soon rendered speech impossible. West's voice was swallowed up by waves of deformity, leaving him to gurgle the saliva-filled sounds of drowning. Tears were pushed out of his crushed eye, and his suffocating jaw only allowed muffled cries. As the disease advanced he found it easier to retreat into silence than suffer the confused looks his grunts evoked. He learnt to exist in dumbness; pen and paper giving him access to the world of symmetrical head and thin face.

3

The stench of vengeance drifts across the stacks of tatty Tower Hamlets, filling the nostrils of those who sleep. East, as he returns to the flat, smells it – the Garners. The police will not be involved; the Garners, a traditional tribe, steer clear of gendarmes – let them protect those who need protecting. An accidental death for Girl will be the suitable verdict, covering a multitude of sins, allowing things to settle, be settled, like decanted wine, blood red.

East is thirsty. In the kitchen, alive with refrigerator hum, water dribbles into an unwashed glass. He sucks at the liquid. West stands in the doorway. East senses him and turns. There is distress in East's eyes, huge and toxic like a boil about to burst. West feels his brother's fear envelop him as morbid aftermath hangs heavy in the air.

– I don't know what to do, East says. – I don't know what to do.

And in those words there is something West has never heard before from East – fallibility. His older brother, for whom life is one lucky dice roll, is uncertain, distant. Never before has West seen him unable to smirk and flash an it'll-be-all-right wink from those invincible eyes.

West is aged twelve, East thirteen, they are walking back from Stepney Green High School. East with his arms around two girls, West following behind.

– Well, see you later, babes, East says, planting a kiss on each girl's cheek before they turn and walk back towards the school.

– Bye, West, they say in unison as they pass him.

East turns to West and grabs him round the shoulders. – Come on, bro, he smiles. – You've got to get that light bulb for Dad.

West has not forgotten, as he did yesterday. Dad was furious and went for the belt. West crept into the kitchen with head bowed, ready to face the punishment, but found Dad sitting at the table and looking across at Mum who was crying. West's lopsided head turned to Dad inquisitively.

– Look, boy, when I tell you to get something you bloody well go and get it, right?

West nodded quickly, aware that the belt was not going to be used.

– Don't think you've got away with it, 'cos you haven't. Trust me, you ain't going to forget again.

West nodded some more.

After leaving the girls, East and West walk all the way to Whitechapel to the nearest hardware store. Shop full of tools, ladders, dustbins, batteries and paint. East takes Dad's note from West and asks the man behind the counter for the bulb.

– No, the man says, hardly looking up from the newspaper.

– You must have one?

– Yeah, you're right, but they're not for sale. He laughs indignantly, nodding up to the light on the ceiling.

East looks to his brother and shrugs. West looks worried.

– Go on, on your way, the man adds sharply.

– Thanks for your help, East says sarcastically.

The man stops reading and looks up. – You better watch yourself, boy.

Outside the shop, West is anxious. He does not want to make Dad angry.

– The nearest other place is up in Bethnal Green. I ain't walking up there.

West's scared eyes nod towards his watch.

– Shit, East says, peering back into the shop. – Don't worry, Westy. Don't worry.

West is not persuaded.

– Worried about a beating?

West nods slowly.

– Don't be. East winks. – If there's a will there's a way.

He picks up one of the metal cans stacked outside the shop and goes back in.

– You back again? the man grumbles.

– I forgot to pick up a gallon of paraffin, East says, handing the man the can.

– Is this one of mine?

– Yeah, I'll settle up with the paraffin.

The man squints and edges through strip-curtains towards the back door and the paraffin tank.

The moment the door closes East grabs a stepladder and climbs up to the light, pulls his sleeve over his hand and unscrews the bulb. West, peering through the front window, shakes his head in disbelief.

– One bulb, East says, triumphantly, handing it to West outside the shop.

West sticks a thumb up, jubilant. He cannot stop patting East on the shoulders as they walk back to the flat.

'Bulb Head' was one of the names that some of the kids from other estates used to call West. Like 'Balloon Brain' and 'Bogeyman' and 'Bubble Face' and 'Beast'. And these were just a few of the words beginning with B.

Mum told him to ignore them and walk away.

East chased after them with a stick.

Dad would get the names and addresses (and then a couple of his mates from the market), and go knock on doors for a 'little chat' with the parents.

4

East tries to shut out the memory of Girl falling and the sirens taking her body away. Beneath sodden sheets, he knows that sleep will not come, yet still he closes his eyes and fights to focus his thoughts on a dream: caressing the chrome levers of a 355, in designer business suit running an empire, undressing Mrs Burdett from the tenth floor. But his mind cannot create, it's full of wasps buzzing and stinging, fears of retribution, memories of Girl Garner.

She was cheap and tawdry with fag breath and grimy fingernails, but she shared her flesh. She had been with East for ten months. She had cash – through the family – and a body, that both seemed to merge for East like the evening's drinking and sulphate, until late, when time for bed, East felt grateful and they found each other's lust. It was a routine, or part of the routine, like going to the Black Horse on the Whitechapel Road. Where they went that last evening.

It has been an ordinary day. East has been to market to offload a consignment of CDs, has popped in for a lunchie at the Lord Nelson in Bethnal Green, has grabbed an afternoon nap, showered, made two phone calls (one to Girl), and now struts to the Horse.

The pub lies cramped between shops, two rusting carriage lights protrude from its grim facade. SALOON BAR on one opaque window, PUBLIC BAR on the other. A single door held open by a brick. It is six thirty, the bars are filling up with natives from neighbouring estates; Willsy, Dawsey, Jerome, Jonesy. End of the day convention for news, debriefs, banter. West will arrive later, so will the rest of the horde.

This is the local, the routine, a pub that stretches back long and thin, becoming darker as you walk from the single door to the toilets at the rear. The bar is along the left-hand side. East sits perched on a stool, running his fingers along the rim of the pint, flicking his head towards Jonesy; nodding, smiling, returning stare to lager.

East turns to Bloke who plays pool with a loose cue that jerks into the balls of those passing to the toilets.

– What's this about a party at Dawsey's?

– Tomorrow. You up for it, Easty? Bloke replies.

– Is Tops going?

– Dunno, why you want to fuck him?

– Crack, crack, what's that noise?

– What do you mean? Bloke asks.

– Oh, it's okay, it's just the thin ice cracking.

– Very funny, little girl.

– Little girls, now you're talking, any going?

– Walk away, man.

East is drinking heavily, enjoying the CD profits. Pushes a twenty into West's hand when he arrives at the bar; clean, dressed in ironed shirt and canvas jeans, black boots, smelling of shampoo. Always a popular arrival, a pat on the back from Willsy, a pint – with a straw – pushed into his hand by Tops. Pen and pad in back pocket for the sporadic note during another night of listening. Another night being one of the lads.

By ten, East is dabbing powder with Tops and Jonesy at a round table opposite the bar. West sucks at a laced drink. The group talk out the energy, West scribbles on his pad. Tonight the wait for his written words is enthralling. Other times it is frustrating and the moment is lost, polite half-smiles greet the scrawled messages.

It's dark outside, the pub has got brighter as the evening has advanced. Clusters stand at the bar, slouch around tables, gabbing over the beats. Willsy is trying to flog a camera to Duke and Jocelyn, the owners, who wave him away with their bar towels. Jonesy leaps from the round table and takes the camera.

– Jones, what you up to?

– Got to try it out before you sell it.

– Take leave, Jonesy.

– Worth some dab?

– Lick length.

– Has it got a film in it?

East throws an arm around West, pulls him into a picture, their heads touching. The flash blows and a strip of black paper slides out from below the lens and shutter. Willsy snatches the camera back before Jonesy shoots another drunken pose. East holds the black paper, now a photo. West does not look. Girl Garner pushes her way to the table holding her half-pint of whisky and water.

– Show me, she insists.

– Prepared to stump?

– Wouldn't you like to know.

She looks at the photograph, closing one eye to focus properly.

– Get the swills, East says to the girl with short black hair standing above him.

– Get the message, she replies, flipping the finger, walking back to her nest of pals at the front of the pub.

– Fuck you! he says.

– Oh yeah? she sniggers, raising an eyebrow.

By eleven, after a battle in front of the lads, East is walking out with Girl Garner. Back to the flat. To the twelfth floor, where West returned early and is now sitting in his bedroom working on a model.

There were other girls East saw, shared, used, at various intervals, in various locations, often in and around the cramped pubs tagged on to the city's estates. The East End was small but distinct districts thrived. From Bow to Shadwell, Globe down to the Island, each corner maintained some identity. United by rampant youth who were free to rave and roam, shaking hands with their common brood, laughing and drinking with fellow rovers, dealing and stealing, feeling tits and naked flesh at each port. Only the fearless had this freedom, most of the inhabitants kept doors locked and curtains drawn, inside by nine, while the bucks roamed the shadows. And there were plenty of shadows in their corner of London. Whole swathes of shade on buildings, railings, fences, roads. The darkness cast by brick towers that drained the inhabitants of colour.

On the bedside cabinet lie the remnants of East's evening: coin shrapnel, wallet (squashed empty), split pack of gum, bunch of keys and the photograph – East and West in the pub. West forced into the frame by his brother's securing arm. West would not have posed voluntarily. He does not like photos or mirrors or windows or blank screens. West does not like reflections. He does not want to know the truth. He shaves what facial hair grows by feel alone. He does not window-shop. He gives his mind as much time as he can away from physical reality. After twenty years of disfigurement there are times when he can forget his face. Precious moments.

In the photo, the glasses on the table are visible, a child's drinking straw of twisted yellow and red stands out of one of the pints. It is, for West, the only way he can drink effectively. The straw is so innocent, so far removed from the panic of death-induced insomnia and the recurring image of the heap of flesh and hair on concrete.

West knocks at the door, enters, sits on the edge of East's bed. East turns away from the photo, lies on his back staring at the ceiling. All traces of amphetamine and alcohol ebb away. Reality dawns, though the sky outside is still cloaked black.

5

West wakes, lying on his side, still on East's bed. Empty. East is standing by the cupboard in the corner throwing clothes into a holdall once used for football boots. There are no suitcases.

West pulls himself up to seated position, ruffles his hair, checks the clock – six. Morning.

– I've got to get out of here, bro, East says, pulling open the top drawer of the bedside cabinet. Driving licence. Passport. Pushed into bag. – They're coming for me, I fucking know it. I'm not gonna sit-arse to find out.

West remains still, only his eyes flicker movement. East looks round, hears the unspoken question.

– I don't know. I don't know where. Some-fucking-where.

West gets up and stands by the window as East studies bits of paper from the drawer. This was home, this had always been home; the five rooms (one they used to share), the ten-mile view over drab rooftops; the streets below that staged and directed their lives. Home to the past – framed on mantelpiece, worn into carpet and curtain, stuffed into cupboards.

No time for reminiscing, time to go. Choosing jogging pants, hooded tops, sweatshirts, jeans, boots, clean skids. East picks at his lips, scanning the room for the obvious, checking under bed, opening top drawer again.

📖 I'm coming with you, West writes.

– No, don't be stupid. You're all right.

West shakes his head and sticks the pad into East's face.

– Look, you can keep an eye on things. Wait for things to die down.

West assumes that things are not going to die down. The Garners do not allow things to die down.

📖 I'm coming.

East sighs an acceptance. Then snaps an order.

– Well get your stuff, we're not hanging about!

East has not left London for seven years. The last excursion was to Southend, as a family. Dad took the lorry. Bank Holiday. End of May. Scorcher. Packed. Dad dressed for winter in jeans and leather jacket as he strolled along the promenade. Mum, in loose cotton, carrying four or five bags full of crisps, juices, cardigans, and creams. Ice creams. Without the flake – I ain't paying that much for a bleedin' thing I can get in the shop next door for half the price! Dad met other day trippers he knew from home, the men dressed for winter, the women with bags. East and West ran off into amusement arcades to play machines. A local kid came up to West and laughed at his face, in his face. Called him a weirdo. East heard the insult and came running, slapped the kid a few times and threw him on to a penny-falls machine, setting the alarm off and sending the kid running out on to the pavement. The family sat in the lorry from five thirty to six thirty in a ten-mile queue. Back along the endless, straight A127, into the city. To home. To Stepney. To the Berserkers.

East's street gang. The Berserkers. East aged fourteen. The uniform of white T-shirt, black jeans, jackets with B insignia stamped on sleeve. Meeting by back steps, by the bins of Blackmore House, one of the three blocks (the others: Compton and Wilton) on a four-acre space ringed by terraced streets and fences, like a stockade.

The gang had about fifty members. Evenings spent sitting

on the steps, smoking blow, listening to the pirates – Dis one gan out to da Stepney massive! – planning action, watching the over-seventeens disappear into cars and on to destinations the gang-youth did not know. Tottenham? Ilford? Islington? Becoming a member, aged thirteen, so he could sit on the steps, wear the B, and swagger into neighbouring estates with a golf club and comrades. How could anyone forget the initiation? It was stamped on his mind as deep as the scar on his arm. A young East, a kid, walking towards the group of boys, a few girls. Taking off his shirt, his trousers, his shoes, a little sparrow of a boy. Blindfolded with his own sweatshirt. Led from steps into building. Junior members standing guard by lamp-posts, by each entrance. His clothes bundled in a heap.

West has packed his clothes with East rushing him. The door to the flat is pulled shut. The brothers are swallowed by the lift, ejected into urine air of ground floor.

For spring, the air is cold. The sky, grey and tired. Carrying the bag over his shoulder, East wants to move quickly. He walks fast, eyes on the pavement, keen to avoid bullet or bat, to avoid falling dead in front of brother, in front of home. It is still early, yet the cars zip along narrow streets. The wide Whitechapel Road on to which they turn moans with the morning flow.

West's knuckles grip white on the holdall's handles, as determined with his hands as he is with his feet that hurry away from all he has ever known. There is an almost perceptible thud of enthusiasm in his steps. He's left behind in his bedroom clothes hung smartly in the cupboard, or folded neatly on shelves. The bed, despite the urgency, flawlessly made. Plants filling the room with oxygen and colour. And on the table there is a model made from matchsticks: a half-finished Canary Wharf tower.

Steps smeared black descend into Stepney Green Underground station. The District, Hammersmith and City lines. Yellow walls, adverts glued huge for films, exhibitions, holidays.

– You okay? East asks.

West nods.

– Can't remember the last time I got on a train.

West shrugs.

– I hate these fucking places.

Aunty Leafy is not a blood relative; 'Aunty' is a title bestowed through familial intimacy. Often at the flat during their youth, sitting in the living room with Sue, sipping tea, stopping round before shopping, after shopping, on her way out. Fitted dresses, messy hair, the smell of talcum powder. Moved out to Essex a number of years ago and became a faceless name in greeting cards. She used to write to Sue on a regular basis, always inviting the family to Basildon for a day out, for a holiday. But by this stage Len was too caught up in things to get away. Aunty Leafy still sends Christmas cards to the boys, and it is West who manages to reply with a short résumé of the year's events (sprinkled with a couple of white ones):

I am well. Haven't found suitable employment this year ... have been offered plenty of jobs ... no point in rushing in. So much to do at home ... tidying, cooking, busy with modelling. Made a St Paul's with paper clips. Okay because plenty of money from East ... small company acquiring CDs – works wth friends ... other pies ... loaded. This time next year the Bahamas! Happy Xmas.

The brothers scuff shoes on the platform, considering what to say to an acquaintance they have not seen for years. A mother stands clasping a baby to her chest. A male in low-slung clothes – denim jeans and sports jacket – struts past with headphones buzzing, nodding his head. EALING BROADWAY . . . 2 MINS. To Tower Hill, then to Fenchurch Street, to Basildon on the overland.

Lights rumble out of tunnel, silhouette in cab. The doors slide apart and brothers, mother, dude enter the carriage. Attention focuses on West's face, then the above-seat advertisements as East stares back defiantly. One child, no older than twelve, keeps his unbelieving eyes on West who sits and pretends to look at the ticket in his hand, avoiding the child's gaze, avoiding his reflection in blackened window.

Behind the blindfold young East reacts to each push and pull as the gang force him against a wall. He can smell his sweatshirt. He can hear feet around him.

– So you want to be a Berserker? Gotta get your brand. Get your print, boy. You ready for that?

Skinny neck rocks a nod. The slight chest heaving.

– You gotta pick for the method. King is fire. Queen is tattoo. Jack is blade. D'ya understand? King is fire, Queen is tattoo, Jack is blade.

East reaches for the cards, grabbing at air, at silence. Makes contact with the slippery slices and takes hold of the King.

Buttons are pressed on aerosols and matches ignited, cans roar flame. A wire fork, bent into a B, is held in the fire. East is tipped to the ground, secured by hands gripping his arms and legs.

The fork glows red. He is not prepared for the agony when flesh hisses and burns. East screams into the jumper now pressed into mouth. Surrounded by faces he cannot recognise, an older girl with black hair watching from behind his haze of pain. He wrestles, tries to fight his way out of the gang's grasp. Unable to break hold, forced to burn.

Above the train, the twelfth-floor flat is peaceful. Neighbours still sleep. There is a noise at the door. The letter box jerks inwards, a dribble of liquid spills on to carpet. The material soaks, swells, a gloved hand directs stream from plastic can through plastic pipe. A match is struck, the hand waits for flame to burst then consolidate. It is dropped through letter box on to sodden floor. A gush of burning.

The train to Ealing Broadway is chattering along dark corridors, sirens above race to a blaze in Stepney. Paint cracks, curtains flood with blaze, and a half-finished model of matchsticks crumples amid the heat.

Hello Goodbye

1

– Where the fuck is this bus stop?

Rain falls as the brothers leave the station. A bus charges through kerbside puddles. Heads, bowed by the shower, hurry past, umbrellas collide, drains gush filth.

– Where the fuck is this bus stop?

They cross the road with a crowd while the green man bleeps, across to a row of bus shelters with timetables attached in glass cases. East asks an anorak.

– Pitsea? Don't know, mate.

He tries someone else; a man in a mac.

– Yeah, pal. You want the number twenty-five, down there on your right.

They told no one of their departure. Mates would talk. They'd probably go to the funeral in borrowed black, watch Mother Garner bawl, eat sandwiches with Father and Geezer, shake hands with Bloke and forget about East and West, on the run, seeking a new life, getting wet under an Essex sky.

The rain is now a torrent as they take their seats on the top floor of the green double-decker, at the front, damp air and windows frosted with condensation. East wipes the wet out of his hair, showering an old man behind who says nothing. West wipes his face with the palms of his hands, as if he is washing. It is the start of the day yet the town is dull under the cloud and rainfall, cars light up the splashing streets with flashes of red and white.

The sauna-bus thrashes through gears, braking hard at each traffic light, the windscreen wipers belting. The route runs between estates, lines of council semis in rusty brick, linked by rows of shops with fading signs. The ceiling, stained by smoke, is decorated with pen. *The Hammers.* TERRY IS A CUNT. *E.W. is rough.*

– How are you? East asks.

West's hair still drips. His clothes are wet. His holdall lies slumped on the floor next to him. He shows an upright thumb. Then, putting finger on window, he draws two matchstick men in the condensation, each with a bag. Above one he writes E, above the other a W. Points to the graffiti. East does not want to laugh but he cannot help it when he sees the stupid picture, the scribbling on the ceiling, the squint in his brother's eye – a smile, definitely a smile.

It is hard to read the face of West, bloated into a single expression. Pain and pleasure often look indistinguishable. Though there are times when slight movements around the clearer eye make sense. It can also be a ruffle of the brow, a twitch of the head, subtle details that transform into language. East knows the signs better than anybody; he is able to read a dilated pupil, a snarl in the jaw.

In the same way, West has grown to understand others through their expressions rather than their words. Trapped within his silence, he is used to observing banter, understanding the power of countenance, paying attention to how words are said. The individual tics, guilty shades of voice and enlarging eyes.

It is this eye for detail that gives West his passion for modelling. A hobby in which he studies the shape, the structure of things. In which he examines the truth of appearance rather than the superficial form. The distinct curve of car panelling. The concave sweep of a ship's bow. The importance of good foundations.

His first model came home in a rectangular box. A Sopwith Camel, complete with transfers and miniature pots of paint. Finished within the hour, daubed brown and yellow and left to dry on windowsill. Each month's pocket money bought a new kit, a new satisfaction, built in the solitude of his bedroom that he filled with plastic planes, cars, ships, tanks, trains, space rockets. Then, the more complicated tasks of churches, skyscrapers, bridges, animals, mountains. On to experiments with modelling materials, learning to create with pencils, cocktail sticks, penny coins.

East did give West time. Time away from seat and table and glue and concentrated stare. Even when a Berserker, East would still throw open the door, shout 'Playtime!' and drag West away from sticks and into the lift, to the world at ground level. Into the community that accepted him as an equal but often failed to treat him as one – it was difficult to talk and tease with a boy whose disease deteriorated with each day. To them he was always the poor kid with the big head, with the funny voice. Even school friends, East's friends, family friends, were unable to communicate without sympathy distorting each sentence, each sigh, each nod, each excuse to walk away.

East saw through the face. He did not ignore it, but he saw through it. They were brothers. Doing things as other brothers did. Leaping from bed at nine during the summer holiday mornings to gorge on cereal before carrying their bikes into the lift and down into the sun for another day. To the market on Stepney High Street to scavenge from the stalls and carry off handfuls of oranges and peaches from the back of the tents while big men with no shirts and loud voices served out front. Playing football with discarded lettuces and bowling rotten apples against walls with shattering explosions of juice. To the chippy for a portion, saveloy, gherkin, in salt and vinegar. Back to the flat for Subbuteo and video games before flicking on television to eat egg sandwiches from blue plates before East slaps empty china on kitchen table and slams front door. 'Later.' Back out, down the lift to join the estate warriors waiting by the steps.

West wanted to join the gang, to hang out by the bins.

📖 Can I go down? he asked Dad, sad eyes behind the notepad.

– Son, you don't want to waste your time with that lot. You've got brains up in the old bonce.

But West knew he was just saying that to keep him in the flat.

📖 You let East!

– He's all over the show, he's not like you.

📖 I'll only go for half an hour.

– You settle down, boy. You've got models and homework and stuff to be getting on with.

📖 I can look after myself. East is there.

– It ain't about you looking after yourself, it's about us looking after you.

West turned away and threw the notepad to the floor.

– It's just the way it is, son, don't start losing your rag with me!

The sound of stomping along the corridor, followed by the bedroom door slammed shut.

– Maybe when you're older! Dad shouted.

Occasionally he got to play football with the gang during the day. Sides were picked and West was added to the team that appeared the weakest.

– You just stay on the wing, his team-mates said. – Just make sure you pass it to one of us.

He stayed on the wing and watched the match ebb and flow and ran into the huddle to celebrate the goals. Then the ball would come to him and he'd trap it, look up, run at the defence. The opposition would let him come at them and dribble around them, while they made half-hearted lunges for the ball. The goalkeeper would dive the wrong way and both teams would cry 'Goal!' and slap his back and lift his arms aloft.

West noticed how their eyes did not shine when he scored, how they did not add his goal to the score.

2

The bus drives over the brow of a hill towards Pitsea. Basildon sits amid the flat expanse east of London, built up with sixties concept housing, encircled by electricity pylons to the north and Thames crane towers to the south. A prosthetic for the Smoke. The address is folded on paper, damp from rain.

Basildon – like Dagenham, Harlow, Wickford, Romford, Grays, and the rest – housed the overspill, housed Tower Hamlets and Newham populations moved under slum-clearance schemes. The Blitz-battered communities torn down to the disgust of some East Enders who did not want the new estates, the new schools, the new gardens promised by developers. Lenny and Sue were among them. They preferred to load their belongings on to a wooden barrow and haul their lives into neighbouring homes and sleep on the floor in spare rooms before the council finished the flats and moved them up to the twelfth floor of Blackmore House. Just as East arrived.

Aunty Leafy stands in the doorway, framed by black. It has been a long time, but she recognises the two boys. She holds out fragile arms. Clawing the bodies to her, clawing the past into her chest. Pushing them back, looking them up and down, and then pulling them back into her embrace.

Leafy's father, Ted, appears as a face in the dark corridor.

– It's Lenny and Sue's boys. You remember them, Dad.

Leafy speaks through dry lips and a cough. Her eyelids sag with her cheeks, and she seems a lot shorter, thinner and weaker than when she was last in their lives.

The house smells of burnt toast and tomatoes. Breakfast just finished, two plates stained red and yolk-yellow sit on draining board, half-finished mugs of tea on the table. More tea for the visitors.

Ted shuffles into the lounge and sits on his chair in the corner, his face melting with time, two trenches down each side of the mouth. The boys deposit their bags in the hallway and follow him into the room, settle on the sofa. Ted is behind them, beside the dining suite, tucked away like a worthless heirloom. Hiding in the shadows of the room keeps him safe, secure among dusty corners.

East receives shouted permission from the kitchen and sparks a cigarette, blowing smoke out of the side of his mouth, away from West. He hurls reluctant chat at Ted, who mutters a single reply, then says no more. East is happy to banter, though not to release clues as to why they have come.

Colin smiles at them. His skin is tanned dark from the

Ibiza sun blazing behind him. He is framed, on the dresser. Tea arrives. East and West drink from floral china, Ted and Leafy from mugs.

– When I lost Colin they moved us out of our big place. We put up a fight but, you know, what with just me and Ted ...

– It's nice, says East, flicking ash into his hand, searching for a tray, searching for the right words to describe the house that seeps sadness.

– Hang on, there's one in the kitchen, Leafy says, noticing the cupped hand.

– Any chance of a drinking straw for West, he adds as Leafy rushes through the door. – It's a bit difficult, you know, straight from ...

– Oh, I'm so sorry. I forgot. I'm really sorry.

The lounge is square, the sofa in the middle facing a fire. Television to the left of the seated brothers, alcove with shelves to the right. On one shelf West notices the Christmas card he sent last year. The card has a picture of Santa on the front, stuck in a chimney with the reindeers laughing. West's handwriting on the inside panels.

– I've got used to the quiet life, Leafy says, returning to the room, trying to justify the smell of loneliness and a mute Ted.

The extended family of five – Leafy and husband Alan, their son Colin, and Leafy's parents, Ted and Ivy – moved into a three-bedroom house together. Part of the migration from Stepney to Essex. The whole street was transplanted as one unit.

One year into the move and Ivy drops dead on the way back from the shops. She falls head first, shattered spectacles rip the face apart. Apples roll to kerb, into a gutter stiff with refrozen slush, the first hands at the scene dip into upturned trolley. Chased away by others, the groceries are saved but it's too late for Ivy. Another year passes before Alan goes. Skips off with Sandra, the woman he saw every day at the bus stop on the way to work. They stood together for two years, seeing the seasons and their lives pass, before they too went. Then it was Colin. Colin's turn to go. It was a terrible day, it was a beautiful day, it was summer. From seven in the morning the sun burnt white and the concrete community smouldered. Dogs scratched around with long tongues, and people lolled from shade to shadow, breathing in melting tarmac. Naked kids, skin stained by Coca-Cola and iced lollies, swarmed about the ice-cream van. The youth lounged in parks, on porches USA-style, and gathered on the picnic benches of the pub.

Colin and company have spent the day on top of a school building; basking, swilling warm beers and whisky. Colin is topless, displaying tattoo on chest – MUM – inside a heart. His body is lean, veins thread the arms. It is getting late, and the evening air absorbs the earlier heat. Ted is asleep in his chair, next to his picture of Ivy. Leafy sits in silence, the television is off for now. As usual, left alone at the end of another day, she drifts back to past times, better times, when Alan was beside her and Colin's head, hair like wool, rested on a knee. Soon be time for the last cup of tea of the day.

At the school, Colin is staggering around, throwing empty cans below. Mum waits for her son. He often gets in at a decent time. He's not a bad boy. Could have been a lot worse, especially now, without a father. He dances to music in his mind, pushing out arms and thrusting hips to the internal beat. He still kisses mum goodnight. It means a lot. That touch. He is standing at the edge. Shouting to the world.

Mum thinks she hears a noise at the door. A key? A slip, that's all it is, a slip and he's gone. Flailing towards the flagstones. Fingers tearing at the sky, feet kicking nothing. Mum stops still, it is not Colin. She thought she heard him.

It aged Leafy, things became hard, things became strange. The months after Colin's death were the worst. When she would not speak. When people in her skull kept going on, making her do things, making her promises. Pills rescued her, and she tried to create a future with Dad, never able to forget all those who had deserted her.

She is upstairs now, rummaging through the airing cupboard for sheets and blankets. Demanding that the brothers take her room; she'll go in with Ted, sleep on the floor. East and West protest, willing to sleep in the lounge. Just a temporary stay. Which gives Leafy more of a reason to offer her room.

– You don't have to rush off. Stay as long as you like, she insists.

Reluctantly, the bags are set down in her room. A room with a pink bedspread, peach curtains, blank walls, and a tidiness that makes it seem like a spare.

Over sausage and chips – Blend it up for you, West? See, I do remember – East gets Leafy to talk names, names arrived from back home, old families, trying to find someone who might remember the brothers, who might know people, who might help.

A splodge of ketchup.

– The Buttons?

– No.

Extra salt.

– The Creeks?

– Name rings a bell.

Sausage sliced in two.

– The Cushions?

Knife and fork stops cutting and prodding.

– You mean Dartford's lot?

Leafy fights West to clear the plates. More tea. West washes dishes, happy to help. Leafy wipes and talks, keen to share every moment, every event of the past years. Letting West's dumbness absorb the outpouring. Alan left Sandra, he is living in Southend. He had a heart attack two years back, last she heard. And then there was Julie, Colin's ex. Julie got herself a new ...

Meanwhile, East is speaking on the phone in the hallway. Got through to Dartford Cushion, old buddy, schoolmate, Berserker, lived on the seventh floor.

– How's West? he asks.

They arrange to meet at the local.

– You boys don't want to go there, Leafy says, her face pinched tight. – It's trouble.

– Where do you drink then, Aunty?

– Oh, we don't get out any more. No good pubs. Not like the Pride. Is it still there?

3

The afternoon sky is filled with cloud, rippled and wrinkled into faces that look down on the brothers as they walk through an alleyway and on a track across a grass verge. Through bollards, past a cluster of lock-ups. The school bell has rung and groups of girls and boys swagger, dressed in precarious uniform. Exhaled smoke blows over earrings and nose studs. The boys loose and sagging; the girls with hair down their backs, and short skirts. The type of short skirt that girls at Stepney School wore, the type of short skirt Girl Garner used to wear.

There are the inevitable pointed fingers as West walks past. A grimace from boys, sniggers from a group of girls. Same old Tobermory, thinks East. But it is the end of the day and the kids want to get away, too tired, too hungry, too schooled-out to spend time jeering at a freak. East struts awkwardly, owing to the swarm of unpredictable kids. He sneers to deter any banter, chewing non-existent gum. Staring at the boys, daring them to speak. Staring at the girls, legs cut so smooth and athletic. Immaculate skin. Pure bodies. Innocent. How he once was.

Margaret seemed so old back then, but she was only forty. The wife of a wide boy, Wally Dennis. She had a brown face and hair dyed squirrel red, brushed across the front, bunched and tangled at the back. As a friend of the family she would come round to drink vodka with Sue in the kitchen, both of them laughing hysterically over jokes, or things other people had said. The boys, unable to get the gags, sat in front of the telly. Always a wink at East and West when she arrived and left. Though when she left, it was always with a bigger smile. Never really spoke, just waltzed through from hall to kitchen, kitchen to hall, a slipstream of scent, her fingers delicately flapping in front of her, or to the side, tapping an invisible keyboard.

When East was thirteen, Margaret and Wally joined Lenny, Sue and the boys on holiday. Two caravans at Clacton. They had spent the day on the beach and returned for a barbecue at the campsite, the two men were out scouring for wood in a pub garden. East and West still in trunks, kicking the beach ball and watching the wind spin and pull it in the air, then blow it off towards neighbouring caravans, tents, bushes.

– Get after it! East would shout, and West would go charging off, carrying his huge head on tiny shoulders.

One time, as it bounced away, East ran into the caravan. 'I'm going to the loo!' Without stopping, eager to return to the ball, he yanked open the door to the shower room. He had not heard the water gushing, splashing over Margaret's body, slapping on to plastic tray.

She is pulling her hair back with the flow from the nozzle, her skin is chestnut from sunbathing on the beach, yet her breasts are spotless white except for the nipples spread dark at the front. Pubic hair dripping in clumps. Thick thighs, brown. Her nose burnt red, peeling from the fall of water. She stands still and watches East gaze at her. So, this is a real woman. Not a mag photo. He runs out to the ball, forgetting why he went to the caravan, why she was in their shower, why he stayed looking for so long.

Nothing was said. Margaret's bikini no longer hid anything from him that holiday, as she ran into the sea or lay on crumpled towel, or bent over to slip on her espadrilles. It would be two years before he saw her naked again.

For mid-afternoon the pub is busy, the same as the Black Horse would be. It is a new building, bright new brick, attached to the housing estate like a porch. The drinkers are all male; feet resting on brass rail at bar, spending the day holding glass. Dartford sees the brothers enter, places his pint on the counter and walks open-armed towards them. He hugs East and then West, taking West's head in his hands and planting a kiss on the swollen skin.

– It's been a long time.

Dartford is still big, his cropped head reaches the glasses

shelf, his powerful arms and torso are wrapped tight in a T-shirt. His dark brown skin and eyes soften his other features; the firm nose and heavy eyebrows. His mixed-race good looks, his body honed on benches pushing steel, on cold mornings putting in the miles, heaving and weaving through hours of bag-work and sparring, make Dartford a different character from so many of the boys they had grown up with. Disciplined, controlled, calm, focused. A man who holds out his hand without a shake, without a tremor. Unlike many – Geezer or Jerome – who do the fitness thing, who do the confidence thing, but conceal their nerves by gripping things harder. Who spend their time making war, making points, making sure people know who they are. Dartford prefers to make friends, make things happen, make the best of a single dad and seven brothers. Four of them are now doing time. Roly, the old man, visits each of them once a fortnight – a fortune in fares.

East still remembered the time when Dartford promised him a pair of old boxing gloves. Another kid at the club offered Dartford cash; at first a fair price, then a good price, then a silly price. Dartford apologised, shook the kid's hand, and passed the gloves to East.

Yet Dartford was no saint, he'd been a Berserker for four years. Liked to rumble with the Bow crews and Bethnal Green brigades. Liked to smoke the weed, drop the Es, pork the judys. He just had standards, ideas about the way things should be done. And, importantly, he had the cool to walk away.

– Sin! I can't even think of the last time I saw you two, Dartford says, collecting change from the barmaid.

– How long you been out here? East asks.

– What, you don't remember me leaving?

East sips his pint, looking away. West notices the tease.

– About four years. Dartford smiles. – We went to Romford for a year but it didn't work out so we moved out a bit further.

– What's it like?

– I tell you, boys, it's wild out here, lots happening. But what about you two drifters, what's up?

– Bit of a long story. Tell you later, yeah.

And the boys settle in for an afternoon. West with his straw, Dartford with his smiles, East with his anxiety, which diminishes with the lagers. And Dartford's vibrations, pulsing assurance and composure into East, who recognises the luck of finding him, a man he can trust. A man who knows, who cares, who can knock on doors.

The three of them sit at a table opposite the bar. The customers around them look the same as in any afternoon drinking stop, like the Horse – old blokes, their arms stained black with ageing tattoos; a fifty-year-old girl with loose skin about the neck, her wire hair moulded into a frizzy helmet, and a voice and a laugh that shatter the drinking calm, sat on a stool beside fellows ten years her junior. The faint red lighting also takes the brothers back to Stepney, but there is something awry. When they have done their drinks there will be no quick walk back to the flat. No casual stroll to the bookies, or Chandi's. East becomes more aware of this after the fourth pint, and the unease manifests itself as a shudder with each swallow. Every slug brings nearer the end of the day.

But West is sitting comfortably, legs outstretched, slouching on the bench.

Dartford leaves for the loo just as entrance the door swings open. Three lads stumble in along with the hum of the outside world. Canvas strides, bright shoes, straggly hairs on top lip and shaved to a point on chin.

– Hello, Bee, one of the lads says, leaning himself against the bar.

– I thought you lot would have had enough last night, the barmaid replies.

There are laughs, though the smiles appear tired, barely clinging to their faces. The first boy digs his hand into his pocket for cash.

– Fuck me, what have we got over there?

The other two look over to East, to West.

– Is he wearing a fucking mask, or what?

– Don't be so cruel, says Bee, holding back a laugh. – He's not bothering anyone.

– Yes he is, replies the first boy, now handling a wad of notes, pulling at them as they hang together in folds. – He's making my eyes hurt just looking at him.

– Well don't look at him, then, Bee says more seriously.

– But he's in my pub. How can I not look at him?

East and West have not noticed the conversation at the bar. The first lad walks over to their table.

– What is an ugly cunt like you doing in my trough?

West stares at the boy. He draws in his legs and pulls himself up to the table. He shakes his head, waving the boy away.

– Hang on a sec, says East, putting down his pint. – That is my fucking man you're talking to.

East jumps to his feet. His teeth bite on his tongue. West reaches out and grabs his arm, pulls him down.

📖 Let it go.

– I asked what's an ugly cunt like you doing in my drinker?

– I'm not going to let it go, Westy. Check this fool, who the fuck does he think he is?

The other two lads stand behind. Bee wipes glasses and keeps her back turned. The rest of the drinkers watch in silence.

West flicks back his head in disgust. East is on his feet, eye to eye with the boy.

– You don't know nothing, pal, says East, spitting it out like a bad taste.

– Oh yeah, you want to end up with a face like that?

– You don't know what way is up, do you, my man?

The toilet door opens. Dartford reappears and notices the bodies standing at the table. East touching noses with another.

– Hey, hey, hey, what's the problem here, Wilson?

Sharing breath with East, Wilson breaks into a cautious grin and raises his hands to show surrender. He steps back.

– Why didn't you say something, strangers?

– No, East says. – I'm not having that. You fucking want a load, now you gotta stay on.

Dartford steps between Wilson and an advancing East.

– I've got enough grief without this cunt giving me static, East says, chopping a hand into his palm.

– Let's compose, guys. There's obviously been a confusion, says Dartford. – Wilson, why don't you guys stroll?

They shuffle towards the door, pull it open to the daylight.

– Put those swills in the cooler, Bee. We'll be back, Wilson says.

West remains seated, shifting his pint about the table, making patterns in the spilt beer. Olympic rings. East is about to lunge, Dartford holds him.

– Let it go, Easty.

– I can't fucking let it go!

– Jeez, you've lost none of the blaze.

4

Roly does not like guests staying over, but after hearing the story of Girl Garner Dartford wangles permission from his dad with a few chosen lies. Dartford remembers the Garners, still hears about them, but decides to help his old friends, particularly when he sees West being dragged along in the wake. He decided it would be safer to stay at his place rather than at Leafy's. The Garners' tentacles are able to slide into Basildon and trace an old family friend of the enemy, in a house alone, without protection. Dartford offers knowledge, offers locked doors and windows to keep out the vengeance.

East is too drunk to walk home to Leafy's anyhow; he's drinking to excess, drowning the pointed finger inside his head.

Dartford's carpet is hard. East's shoulder aches from lying sideways. He tries to roll over but finds himself knotted in the sheets that he shares with West. East reaches for the jug of water by his side and slurps at it. Dartford lies flat on his bed, a plank of mahogany. Four hours' kip for East, not enough, not nearly enough, but he's wide awake with the delirium tremens and longer-term concerns.

He wants to get a drink but cannot face stirring from the makeshift bed. He wants to ask West to go and fetch a pint of milk or a can of Coke from the kitchen downstairs, but he is reluctant to wake his brother who sucks and gurgles beside him. As he did when they shared a bedroom for so many years. When Dad would sometimes appear in the middle of the night.

East, aged twelve, lies in bed half-asleep, listening to West struggling to breathe. The snorts and splutters are more desperate than usual and cause East to get out of bed and go to his brother. Gently, he tries to move West on to his back, and he pulls at his cheek hoping to open the airways to his nose. West groans and jolts and East pulls his hands away to watch his brother fade back into sleep. They have both had a busy day with Dad on the lorry, then with family arguments after tea.

The boys kept their heads down in the living room and pretended to watch television until Sue pushed open the door and pointed at them.

– What about your sons? What about them? she shouted.

West rolled over on the settee. East just rolled his eyes and shook his head.

Lenny left at eight in the evening for a job in South London. Sue screamed at him not to go.

– You've got responsibilities! she shouted.

– I'm going to be all right, Lenny yelled back, slamming the front door as he left.

Back in bed that night, East sees the light from the landing stretch into the room as the door is pushed open. It is two a.m. and Lenny creeps in, still wearing his coat and boots. He is slightly out of breath and East can hear that he is struggling not to pant. With the light behind him, he seems huge. East sits up.

– Dad?

West, too, stirs, always tuned into Lenny's late-night visits.

– All right, lads? Dad asks, using the words to catch his breath.

West pulls himself up and waves from his corner of the room.

– Well done, Dad, is all East says, happy to have him back home after the row earlier.

– Mum's all right, don't worry, I've had a word, Lenny whispers, standing in the middle of the room.

– Is everything okay? East asks.

Lenny lets out a slight chuckle. – Yeah, everything is top and tailed.

He is just a silhouette, giant-like as his slightest movements are enhanced by the darkness. He lowers himself on to the floor to sit; the clump of boot and rustle of donkey jacket. The room smells of sleep and pyjamas, the brothers turn on to their sides to watch Dad.

– Look, lads, he says, reaching into his coat and pulling out a pile of cash. – I want you to have a little bit of loot, you know, for today's work. You were a great help.

From the wad he flicks off a few notes and passes them over to East, then West.

– Now slip that under your pillow and don't tell your mum, right?

Lenny pushes himself up and makes for the door. Back in the wedge of light he turns around. He stands there in silence while the brothers sink under the sheets.

– You're good lads, he says, disappearing behind the closing door.

Dartford burps.

– More tea, vicar, East whispers, testing to see whether Dartford is awake.

There is no reply and East puts his hands behind his head to stare at the grey ceiling. Thinks about the pub earlier, the three lads, running through various scenarios. The obvious move; glass broken on table and slammed into face. Or fingers thrust into eyes and followed with fists to cheek and jaw. Or knee to bollocks. Or a dummy lunge, pushing Wilson on to the back foot, edging him towards the bar where a one-two manoeuvre would land him head first against the wooden counter, to be grabbed by hair and smacked on to ledge, into broken nose and unconsciousness.

West's eyes flicker yet cannot stay open. East remains on his back, staring upwards.

It was Margaret who, two years after the holiday, arranged for East to come round and pick up a coffee table for Sue. She opened the door of her terraced house in Clinton Road, and shut it after a furtive glance outside, at the street, at the empty driveway. She wore a translucent blouse, naked underneath, allowing her full breasts to push against the material, giving East another view of her maturity. She smelt more exotic than usual, the perfume was different, the scent of somebody else. She led him to the living room and sat next to him, close. East was a Berserker but he could feel his legs wobbling, he kept swallowing stale saliva.

– Can I get you anything? she asked, smiling.

– No, no, I'm fine.

– You sure?

She brushed her hands over her skirt.

– You're getting so big, she said, looking him up and down.

East grinned politely. – Yeah, I guess.

– I hear you're a bit of a hit with all the girls at school.

She kept smiling, kept her eyes fixed on him as if she was trying to say something else.

– Look at those muscles, she said, gently pressing his biceps and letting her fingers slip along to the elbow. – I can see why you get all the girls.

East remained quiet. With the gang he knew the deal but there, with Margaret, he felt lost. He knew Wally. He didn't want to misread things.

– Are you sure there's nothing I can give you? she said, turning her body to face him, her boobs rubbing against his arm.

He wanted to look down at her breasts but it would seem so blatant. He offered a raise of the eyebrow, a slight shrug.

– I don't know, he said.

Her breath filled his, she stretched her arm along the top of the sofa, fingers tinkering with his black hair. East felt his eyes glazing over. Then she pushed her lips against his. Her arms pulled him closer. She took his hands and placed them on her chest. She sighed, he swallowed. Woman and boy embracing. Woman and boy touching. She slid out of her skirt, her tights, and flicked open his buttons, yanked off his jeans. To the bedroom. She leading, he staring – staring at her wobbling buttocks as they climbed the stairs.

He never told anyone about Margaret. It was too risky, too personal. Unlike the later shags that became public property, Margaret was his experience alone. There is comfort in remembering, in closing his eyes and hugging the past. Fifteen miles downstream and certainty has faded. Away from the familiar, life has lost its definition and shape.

East likes to talk about a hard childhood whenever he meets strangers or shares a pint with a new face in the Black Horse. But it was not hard – it was easy. Embraced by the community, initiated into the Berserkers, seduced by adults. This was nothing more than the avuncular hand of the East End ruffling his hair, letting him know that he was loved, that he was one of the family encamped on the northern shore of the Thames.

The Berserkers had mottoes: 'Eat Them Alive', 'Mad and Bad', 'Never Stray'. Too many times gang members were caught on the wrong side of the Whitechapel Road, buying crisps in the Londis on Globe Road, or getting an ice cream from Angelo's Pizza Parlour on Cambridge Heath.

The Colts (named after Three Colts Lane) of Bethnal Green liked to consider Angelo's part of their terrain. Dressed in denim jackets with horse heads sewn on the back, the gang congregated outside Angelo's during the warmer months, leaning against the windows of neighbouring shops and concealing weapons in their pockets.

Tops had been playing football for the Borough; he always travelled to the match in his lucky Berserker's uniform. Dropped off on Bethnal Green Road when he missed his lift to Jamaica Street, decided to walk it back. Eat Them Alive. Arrived home three weeks later after he ran into the Colts, grazing on the pavement, who attacked him with claw hammers. Two of the blows fractured his skull. Six broken ribs. Ended his football season early. Though the Berserkers evened the score in the rematch – the home tie.

Never Stray. And here he was, stuck in Basildon without a gang. Without a plan. Waiting for morning to come. Dartford belches again, mumbles an apology, adjusts the duvet. West's eyes creep open, the thick curtains keep the room in dusk.

It was so easy spending years not having to think, not having to confront dilemmas. The issues were simple: What time to get to the pub? Whether to work in a suit or dabble with the boys? What to have for breakfast? How much to spend on a new hi-fi? What shoes? Mere extensions of the questions asked earlier in life: Whether to bunk off school? Where to smoke that joint? How to get out of the washing-up? What to do with Dartford's boxing gloves?

The only time he had to think was when he made his regular trip to Mum and Dad's grave. A shared plot in Mile

End behind Clements Hospital. The brothers never visited together; each one wondered what the other did there alone.

East does not understand mourning, does not know what he is meant to do. He stands by the grass mounds and looks at other headstones. No one told him whether it is better to cry or be strong and so he stays by the plot pretending to do neither, watching contrails from passing aircraft zip up the sky. Occasionally he chases off kids who scratch names on the stones and leave litter. But the cemetery is just outside the comfort of the parish and he likes to get back.

West relishes the trips to see Mum and Dad. In the peace and seclusion of the graveyard, he takes out his gardening tools and clips at the grass. Digs out an edge. Scrapes away muck. Kneeling or sitting cross-legged, after his gardening duties, he talks to his parents, internally, waits for a reply. West designates a reply as any specific sound breaking the silence. A bird call, a distant car horn, a cracking twig, a shout. Each will satisfy, and this allows the deformed boy to stand up, bow his head for a minute, and walk towards the gate.

Holed up in his room, after sweetened coffee and toast, they await the return of Dartford. It is midday. Dartford has spent the morning on the phone, touching base with contacts. It has been difficult for him because people want to know details: what happened, who is running and, more importantly, who is chasing. Dartford knows that the name Garner will scare away help. He is on thin ice; one crack in the conversation and receivers are replaced. East phones Leafy. She is waiting for them and wants to know when they are coming back.

Dartford returns at two o'clock and calls for a taxi. The three of them leave the house, stand at the end of the road, checking their watches.

– Just ask for Noel when you get there. Say I sent you.

– Is he cool?

– He won't let you down. Stick with him and you'll be all right. Noel's the man.

Dartford stays on the pavement as the car pulls away. West gives a quick salute then turns to face front. East, with his arm laid across the back seat, keeps his eyes fixed on Dartford, looks at him for the last time.

Out Coming

1

Leafy stands by the door in a bright dress, anxiety etched into her face, twisting a tea towel in her hand. East clumps up the stairs; West passes Leafy and offers a sympathetic shrug. They stuff their bags, check the room. Leafy appears at the door.

– What's going on?

– It's nothing, Aunty. Honest. Something's cropped up.

– I told you that pub was trouble.

The ringing phone interrupts and Leafy picks it up in the bedroom.

– Yes, he's here. I'll just get him. She turns to East. – It's for you.

– Who is it? Ask who it is.

– Who's calling?

East's face burns, he stares at Leafy, waits for answer.

– He says it's a friend.

It is someone who spoke with Dartford this morning. Who was unable to help the brothers at first, but has now come up with a plot. He is a friend from way-back-when who's now making his way in the flatlands. He wanted to surprise East, but East does not take the receiver. For East thinks it is the Garners. For East, the Garners are calling, the Garners are closing.

– Hang up!

– Pardon?

– Hang up!

A peck on the cheek, a hug for Leafy from West, and the two brothers are back in the taxi. Bags on back seat.

– Don't leave me, Leafy says. – Stay longer.

Wringing the cloth as she stands alone on the front step. Shaded doorway behind her, she waves at the boys driving off into the sunlight that is breaking through cracks in the afternoon cloud.

– Don't leave me.

The taxi driver is called George; he sits on a bead cover, flicking his cigarette into a full ashtray. The brothers study his neck, pockmarked and scarred, as he drives them to Noel's.

– I hope you know where you're going, East says.

– Yeah, I know, George replies. – Everyone knows Noel.

Noel, too, has a noteworthy face, so the brothers have heard. They're immersed in the memorable. Unforgettable faces, unforgettable memories, unforgettable deaths.

West's class at primary school did not want to be forgotten. They chose ten objects that represented modern life – their modern lives – and each wrote a short note to the future, which they shut in a biscuit tin to be buried at the city farm opposite the school.

A picture of the class. A one pound note. A Biro. A can of Coke (empty). A CD of the top ten singles in the pop charts.

Hello. My name is William and I live in London. I am ten years old and like football, fried chicken and running. When I am old I want to be a man who drives floats at carnivals. I have a mum and two sisters who annoy me. I hope you are having a nice time in the future.

A Mars bar. The front page of a newspaper. A first-class stamp. An electric plug. A magazine picture of the Royal Family.

West's note was not like William's. Or Maxine's, or Brenda's, or any of the others. His note was not about him but what it was like to be him. Mrs Edgar, the class teacher, didn't notice West swap the approved copy for a new version while the tin was being sealed.

The earth was hard, crusty, and the children took it in turns to pick away at the soil with hand-held forks and spades. They were unable to create a big enough hole until help came from an employee of the farm who lunged at the ground with a rusty pickaxe and spade.

The grave gaped at the feet of the gathered class, their trainers were smattered with mud. And as the biscuit tin was placed in the hole, West could not withhold a crumpled grin. A drum roll of soil as it falls on to the metal container.

For West, school became a frustration, a place where he was forced to compete by his obstinate parents and the acquiescent staff. The more his voice disappeared into his flesh, the more he was urged to speak up, talk louder, shout. He ended up screaming with printed words on paper.

He passed all his exams but was passed over by the gangs. Considered staying on at school and trying for A levels, but the family needed him for work by the time he was sixteen – money was scarce. He read through the jobs pages with Mum, and wrote a handful of letters to adverts for vacancies. Received a number of rejections, a couple of positive responses. Never forgotten the job interviews.

Dad's got him a new suit, off a friend in the rag trade, business closing down, good gear. A bit short in the leg, too much sock on view. A bit long in the jacket, it hangs over West's small frame.

– You look like a clown, East jokes.

– Shut it! Dad rebukes.

West stands still while his parents pull lapels and tug at sleeves. Push the tie up, tight. Their boy is going out into the world, going to do them proud – 'what with all his brains'.

His thick folds of skin are polished and Dad has given him a proper shave; he slid the razor into facial trenches, lifted mounds of skin with one hand while wielding the blade with the other. He stood West in front of a mirror to perform the task and did not notice his son's closed eyes; his head facing forward, unmoving, with eyes shut.

Eau de toilette slapped over jaw and cheeks, West is baptised by his father into the morning rituals. Now Dad brushes him down with the palms of his hands before opening the door. Watches the small body with its swollen head limp towards the lift.

West hops on the District line, to Victoria.

At the office he is asked to sit in the foyer. The receptionist relays his arrival into the phone, her smooth demeanour betrayed by a twitching pen and, after the call, tuneless humming. West flicks through a business magazine, trying to regulate his breathing, ease the sweat. Glossy images of good-looking grins, perfectly formed business faces – hurrying about offices, sitting on airlines, shaking hands. Shaking hands on a completed deal, on a completed scheme, their completed lives, complete bodies. West replaces the magazine on to the pile.

– Good exam results. Well done.

West nods, accepting the compliment. His hand grips pen and clipboard – both specially bought for today – with sheets of A4 attached under a metal rod.

– Did you find your dumbness a hindrance to study?

West shakes his head, is about to write a more complete

answer, ready to shake off nervousness and display his ability to communicate, when another question comes.

– Can you type?

West shakes his head.

– Use a PC?

West looks up from the paper and shakes again.

– Can you sign-read?

The twelve stops home on the Underground took an age. His parents' disappointment was hidden behind encouragement. – You'll show them next time, son. They don't know nothing.

East shrugged. – Bad luck, Coco.

West's room remained drenched in the scent of the eau de toilette. Every night for a week he breathed in his failure.

The second interview was worse.

Tube to Earl's Court. Management trainee position. Dad accompanies him on the journey and they arrive early. They find a café and Lenny buys him a cup of tea, then waits with the paper while his son makes his way to head office.

West returns twenty minutes later, his head bent on to his chest. Resigned. Glad to be away from the overweight man in the suit sat in that bright room. Those last words of his, West heard in a haze.

– It's not the dumbness, it's the face ... will upset other members of staff ... and clients ... All the best for the future.

West writes out the words for Father. Adds at the end:

📖 It's no use, Dad.

The street is busy with office workers, shoppers, tourists. Lenny is dragging West behind him, pulling him over, pulling him up, dragging him on. Passers-by stare but do not get involved. Into head office. The secretary is reluctant;

Lenny is insistent. The man from the bright room arrives with outstretched hand. Lenny throws a right to his chin, snapping his head sideways; the man crashes head first to the floor.

– You are not going to destroy my son!

As he drives, George chats away harmlessly, telling the brothers about his days as a sinner, about his days as a player in the criminal underworld of East London and Essex. East reels off a list of possible contemporaries: Tony Dark, Ronnie Poland, Wally Dennis, the old man.

– I knew faces rather than names. That's how it worked back then, George says.

East's suggestions undermine George's credibility, and the driver slides the conversation into the present.

– So what 'appened to your boat, pal?

– He finds it hard to speak, mate, East replies.

– I'm not bloody surprised.

– It's a disease.

– Hope it's not catching! he says, laughing with choked lungs.

Two heads in the back seat turn to look out of windows.

They leave behind the wide avenues and roundabouts of Basildon. Hit countryside, trees and hedgerows, gates. Smoking chimneys in the near distance.

– Not far now, lads.

– Right.

– You on the run? Is that what all this is about?

– Don't really want to say, you know what I mean.

– I do know Noel personally. I've had plenty of people like you in the back of the car.

– Don't really want to say.

– Well, don't get me wrong, but you ain't gonna get yourselves too far with a boat like that. It's a sore thumb, pal. A sore thumb.

West hadn't even considered that his loyalty to East could jeopardise his brother's getaway. But what if he had stayed behind?

Stepney was home, that was its advantage – he knew the roads (Jamaica Street, Smithy Street, Oley Place . . .); he knew the faces (Tops, Jerome, Jonesy . . .); the shops (Aldred's, Leach the Butcher, Slatcher's Fruit and Veg . . .); the smell of Stepney Way on a Sunday afternoon (shitty, metallic); the view from the twelfth (insipid, endless); the sound of the school bell at Blue Coats (scary). A place as small and selective as Stepney gave West some kind of security. And Stepney was small. West and East proved this years earlier when the two of them engraved a fifty pence piece with their initials, either side of the Queen's head. Tiny flecks of metal ploughed up by a compass point. E. W. They spent the coin in Aldred's, got it back in Slatcher's a week later. Half a chicken from Leach and the coin slotted back into circulation. Took it off Bloke in the Black Horse when Duke tipped a pile of change on to the bar. Left it on the pavement outside the bookies. Two days later True Colours came in at five to one, the fifty pence came in as part of the profit.

Stepney was home, that was also its disadvantage – it was memory, it was past, where he was Lenny's lad, the lovely boy with the disease. It was home to the time capsule. Buried.

West remembers the biscuit tin as they pass green fields. He recalls how he wanted out of the project, wanted out of polite back slaps and forced 'one of us' salutes, wanted out of the amphetamine scene – too easy for him to watch Tops' powder float in the glass, to suck and feel good until the morning when happiness was gone, replaced by hollow self-analysis that neither East nor the others seemed to suffer. So many mornings West declared an end to sulphate consumption only to have East laugh at his intentions; unable to believe that anyone would genuinely wish to abandon the thrill of whizz, the thrill of Tops reaching over the table.

West saw his own malleability as a weakness. Though he drew comfort from the fact that he possessed enough self-control not to indulge in the full menu enjoyed by the majority of Black Horse drinkers. These chemicals were usually consumed during fortnightly excursions to the West End that he chose to forego. Left behind to open the door to returning troops who dragged their way home in ones and twos with stained shirts, penniless pockets, scarlet eyes. On trains, on night buses, in taxis, walking. With the shakes, without the shakes. With female, without female. Back to the brothers' flat to tentatively sip at coffee, to sleep, to regroup and recount events.

Tops – on the floor, legs stretched out, face made blank by incoming sunlight. Smiling through illuminated dust. White, five foot ten, ring in each ear, muscular. A loud laugh. Always joking. Two years' chokey at sixteen. Young offender. Life spent waiting for the break to happen. Meanwhile, happy for casual work in the building game, sign on, make cash from wherever.

Jonesy – on the floor, back pushed up against sofa. Second-generation Jamaican, six foot, sportsman. Still jogs. Works for an insurance firm in the City. Wants to chuck it in, set up his own business. Or travel.

Bloke – sitting in the armchair, feet on the coffee table, taking the piss. Says what he wants to who he wants. The youngest of the Garners. Hair greased back, lapping against the gold chain round neck. Works for the family.

Jerome – mixed-race Lanky. Enormous hands. Perched on a chair at the table opposite West, laughing with Bloke. Laughs and agrees with everything Bloke says, thinks, does.

West has to suffer silently as they toke blow and joke about the previous night's fights: how Bloke broke a window, broke a nose – the nose of a tanked-up broker pushing at the bar. How Tops and Willsy swapped fists with two Geordies. How Jerome swiped glass into a doorman's face.

Or the evening's catches – the girls from West London, from the South Coast, from north of the border, the tourists, au pairs, students. East would often appear in the living room with a catch, he in his pants and T-shirt, she in his gown. Holding mugs. Always the same; the girl with feet turned inwards, hair fluffed up from the pillow, her mouth red and irritated from the night's contact. East never denied West an introduction: the girl normally smiling and then dipping her head into a steaming drink; West lowering his gaze back on to a model he fixes and shapes, assailed by smoke and stories.

Andrea, Colette, Fanny, Holly, Ingrid, Maria, Marie-Helene, Nancy, Naomi, Tanya, Victoria. And the others. They all began to look alike to West, sitting by his model after a night alone, using tweezers for delicate procedures. Just some of the girls made a mark. Ingrid with long legs and hairy pits; Marie-Helene with huge breasts; Colette, cocoa brown, skirt skimming the white panties. West couldn't help remembering them as he glued, their images sticking to his mind.

The boys joked about the sex, the girls, the violence. Not too funny for West who has only touched the one girl – Karen Trimble.

Karen Trimble of Wilton House. Four years ago now. East's last year as a Berserker, West was sixteen. A birthday party arranged at the flat while 'the parenthesis' (Mum and Dad) were out for the evening. It was generally agreed that it was time for West to get laid.

Karen hangs out with the Berserkers. She is fifteen, swigs from the cans, smokes, lets the boys put their hands up her skirt. She goes around with a group of girls referred to as the 'Twat Pack' by the gang. Girls can't become Berserkers, but they can sit on steps and listen to the bull and bravado of adrenalin, of the nitrate-fuelled males who call the estate theirs.

A few of the girls have earned respect for stealing, for stabbing, for fighting teachers at Green High. They carry weapons on fight nights, push puff into pants, get naked. Most are happy to tag along behind the boys who make plans. Like Karen. Who spits. Who lives in Wilton. Who calls Jonesy her 'real boyfriend'.

– I can't do it, Karen insists.

– How about a BJ?

– Why can't Janey do it?

– Listen, I want this party to go with a bang, says Bloke. – And I mean a bang.

Jerome laughs loud, laughs to please Bloke.

The other girls, happy not to have been selected, join in the persuasion. Most of the gang are sitting on steps watching the dispute. Karen's desperate appeal shouted over by Bloke and the girls. Jonesy stays silent, does not want to stand in the way of hierarchy. He smokes a cigarette, turns away. Karen's argument is spoken to the wall of the block, to the wall of Bloke's authority. She knows that the gang is too important, too powerful. She falls quiet, knowing that the twenty-five faces staring at her expect obedience. Bloke grins. Jerome grins. Karen takes a bottle of wine and swallows.

2

Noel's house is shrouded by trees, by a brick wall topped with razor wire that runs the length of the garden. Two black gates stand before the brothers, an intercom is attached to the side walling. A shingle driveway, edged with chunks of stone, sweeps out of sight through the railings between tree trunks and bushes.

The sky is a mix of black and white, crisp air floats from the bordering foliage, darker scents from the road and nearby Thames – the dour breath of industrial water. East shrugs his shoulders at West and presses the button. Uncertain, the brothers wait for a response, trying to glimpse a welcome through the bars. The gates crunch into movement, gliding, then stuttering apart.

East strains to recognise himself as an absconder. He remembers how he met with indifference East End colleagues on the run from the Law. How he pretended concern and ordered a pint and waited for the guy to hit the road. He offered help, offered a score, but ultimately left the runner on his own.

Then there was Ralph, just jumped Scrubs, dripping desperation on Jonesy's settee, awaiting the call from the haulage firm who were willing to slot him inside furniture and ship him to the continent. Ralph sat squirming in Wormwood strides – institution blue with a smattering of pockets – and checked shirt, while Jonesy, Bloke, Tops and East brushed hairs off their clothes and dust off armrests, keeping their eyes away from Ralph's, brushing him off with silence and a mug of untouched tea.

– Wouldn't like to be in your shoes, pal, said Bloke at one point, head resting on back of chair.

Quite often a stranger passed through the Stepney shadows

on his way out of the city, leaving behind nothing but the relief of those who didn't have to be the runner, who didn't have to skulk away into minicabs with unwashed hair and ripped jacket. Who didn't have to leave the comfort of bar stool and bar buddies, own life, own bed. No, East did not see himself as one of those wrecks who startle at a ringing phone. At a ringing doorbell.

The front door is striped with metal bars, a sliding spyhole opens; East and West the prisoners stand outside. Steel thumps shut, a clank of turning lock, the heavy door edges inwards. A woman in a red suit waves them into a spacious hallway – wide stairs curving up one side, paintings smartly pressed against walls, side tables replete with crafted ebony and glass. West, the matchstick and cocktail-stick craftsman, marvels at the art. East puts down his bag in the middle of the floor and looks at himself in a mirror by the door. Haggard eyes stare back, there's growth on cheek and jaw.

The fugitive faces nod at Noel, who sits behind a desk in his study. The woman leaves the room without a word or eye contact. The room is full of artefacts and framed pictures, but the brothers' eyes are not on its contents. They are on Noel and the two scars that run up either side of his face. Mouth to ear, left and right. A Sicilian smile. Noel wears a turtleneck and sports jacket. A thin cigar points from his mouth, behind him a window overlooks an extensive lawn and a tennis court. He wipes his hands across his white hair that clusters in lumpy strands, leaving areas of scalp bald. Little eyes peer out of the reptilian face. He has seen action. Now, though, he's comfortable in the secure abode from which he runs his business; pinching lips on the brown stick, waiting for the red lady to close the door.

Noel offers the boys a drink, stepping from desk to cabinet.

Able to stroll to glass and decanter, to sense the brothers' impatience. To watch them sit incongruous amid rich decor.

West tries to pour the single malt into his mouth, unwilling to ask a man like Noel for a drinking straw. It trickles from his twisted jaw on to his jacket, and he attempts to bite the glass into position. East is too nervous to concern himself with his brother's dribble. He's trying hard to appear indifferent, in control, swirling the glass around, punctuating the circular motion with sudden throws of liquid on to his tongue.

– Don't worry, son. I know what it's like to be fucked up. When they carved my face I was on liquid for a month.

His voice has a sharp edge. It sounds younger than he looks.

East holds back the last gulp, readying himself for the final burn, allowing it to sink down his throat with a backwards roll of the head. The booze from last night has left him; the whisky is a welcome tonic. It would normally be a hair of the dog at the Horse, but times are different now.

– He's a good lad is Dartford. He made a real effort for you two. But, as I told him, I'm not a charity. Before we go any further I need you to flash the cash.

– How much?

– Well, considering Dartford pulled in a favour – a small one, mind you, I don't owe big ones – we'll call it a grand.

East turns to West, pulls up his top lip and expands his eyes.

– We don't have that much.

Noel reaches for his tumbler and sips, sucking in air through his teeth.

– Look, I can see you're good kids, I want to help, I do, but

I've got to run things, you know? He strokes the side of the glass. – Okay, okay, call it eight. Eight is great, on the slate.

– We haven't got eight. We've only got about five.

– All I can do is give you till tomorrow morning. I've got things to sort out.

– How am I going to get an extra three ton?

– My friend, all I can do is give you till tomorrow.

– What time tomorrow?

– Just be early, eh?

Karen Trimble is dancing to the music that plays in the living room, three hours after swallowing her first slug of wine. The other girls dance even more deliriously than usual, free from obligation. East stands against the sink in the kitchen, necking a can of lager, winking at Bloke as West watches the dancing, straw in mouth.

It is nine thirty. The parents are returning at about midnight and the gang await Karen's move. Nine thirty at a Berserkers' party was usually the time for couples to pair off, to share a can, bottle, spliff, to find a room, doorway, cupboard in which to have sex. But tonight people are anticipating the arrangement. Every conversation is overwhelmed by the shared secret in a roomful of eager eyes.

Karen, in a tight top and leggings, is next to West offering a birthday kiss, barely able to speak through the alcoholic fog she has induced. West does not notice the surreptitious stares as he dances close to Karen, the general smell of hashish and sweat replaced by the more intimate scent of oily hair and streetwise skin. Her hands touch West and stroke his neck and shoulders. The first caress, his first embrace, yet he is unable to kiss. She moves closer and pecks at his throat. With her mouth on him she can almost forget who he is. Regular sex with Berserkers has made her body respond automatically, with closed eyes, and imagination. She often finds herself sat astride, bent over, pulled apart, her mouth stuffed full. Sensual moments are saved for Jonesy. Though he too has had to wait his turn in the past. Sex within the gang is a different currency, it belongs to the group like a member, like loyalty.

Inside his room West sits on the edge of the bed watching Karen undress. Inner-city eyes and pasty skin, bruised arms. Yet the breasts are sculpted on to the chest, taut and naturally balanced, and symmetrical bones protrude from shoulders and hips. As she peels off her remaining underwear, West pulsates with near orgasm as he sees the narrow thighs and trimmed pubic hair.

When the door opens again West feels clean despite the mess of unprotected intercourse, and there is a sense of being light, bright amid the cacophony of celebration. Under which no one hears Karen clutching at her clothes and locking herself in the bathroom.

By midnight the flat is clear of cans, roaches, Berserkers. East is back out on the estate, their parents back in front of the box. West lies in bed thinking about Karen, intoxicated from the beers, the sex. Amazed how he struggles to remember her shape, her aroma, even her underwear that he had studied so carefully. West sits up in bed and looks about the floor in case she has forgotten any items of clothing. He pulls the duvet around his face to breathe in those moments, but she has gone, all that is left is the odour of cigarettes and polyester. And a butterfly-shaped stain on the undersheet.

Morning brings a clearer mind, even though he's fighting the effects of a hangover. He looks over to East and smiles at the legs and arms spilling out of his bed. Laughs as his brother wakes with a start and mumbles words incoherently.

– You okay there, bro? East groans.

West raises a thumb and lies back on his pillow looking smug.

– And now you're a man, East says, rearranging his duvet and pulling it over exposed limbs.

West blows on his fingernails and pretends to wipe them on his chest.

East snorts a chuckle. – I knew I was right to go with Karen.

West turns to his brother.

– No, nothing, East says, dismissing West's stare with a flick of the wrist.

The truth of his seduction begins to appear. West recalls Karen leaving the party soon after, without a kiss or a word. Too happy to notice at the time but now her departure says something. West climbs from his bed and goes to stand by East.

📖 What do you mean – you were right?

– Forget it, Westy. Just forget it.

📖 Are you telling me that you told her to do it with me?

West had heard about things like this before among the Berserkers, but he didn't think that East would play a stroke like that on him.

– Oh, come on, bro. It's way too early for all this.

📖 Tell me, I want to know.

– Loosen up. It's just a bit of harmless fun, take it easy.

📖 You made her?

– It was a pressie, don't tell me you didn't enjoy it.

His success had become a failure. It had become humiliation. He wanted sex, East knew that, but West didn't want it given to him like a charitable donation; the chorus of 'Happy

Birthday' that had broken out when he emerged from the bedroom like the rattle of coins in the collection tin.

📖 It was unfair.

– You weren't complaining last night.

📖 I didn't know last night.

– What did you think she was doing? You couldn't have thought she was doing it for real.

📖 For real? Cheers!

– Ah no, Westy, I don't mean it like that. You know what I'm saying.

West throws on some clothes and leaves the flat, makes his way to Wilton House. It is Friday morning and the blocks are emptying for the day. West sits on the rails outside so he can see into the hallway. The chill of November, the metal bar branding his thighs with cold, patches of ice on the path. Kids in school uniform barge their way through the doors, followed by mothers and prams, followed by Karen. Her legs wrapped in black stockings for school, a scuffed pair of clodhoppers, a blue jacket buttoned up to her chin. He moves off the rail, she does not look at him, maintains her casual pace, avoiding the patches of frost.

West is ready with a note, and as she approaches he takes it from his pocket with numb fingers. She forces a polite smile, unwilling to compromise the Berserkers' plan, yet equally unwilling to encourage West's affections. She stops next to him and West reads uncertainty and fear in her expression. He reaches out to touch her on the arms to reassure her. Karen's body stays still yet her face jerks to one side. West retracts his hands and steps back. He holds out the envelope. He nods at it. She picks it out of his cold fingers. She smiles at the pavement and walks to school.

The gates are open, pupils sloping through to a playground

full of squeals, footballs, and clusters of coats and black uniforms blowing steam. Karen opens the envelope before she reaches the gates.

📖 I did not know. I'm so sorry.

She walks past the gates, past the wire fencing, a voice shouts out.

– Karen Trimble fucked a freak! Karen Trimble fucked a freak!

The brothers need to get to a phone; West remembers passing one in the taxi. It was a few miles back towards the town. They walk, bags slung over shoulders. East sticks out a thumb but no cars stop, rushing past. One or two sound their horn as a jeer.

– Wankers, says East.

The weather has turned cold, the late afternoon brings a damp breeze. It clings to the boys who zip up their jackets and continue to walk.

Set back from the pavement on a grass verge is the telephone. A wooden fence runs behind the booth, sealing off the houses with backs turned to the road. Already muted lights shine through closed curtains, the warmth of home, socked feet on carpet. East slips Dartford's number out of back pocket, pushes in a few coins and waits for reply.

Roly answers. Dartford is not in. Has not been seen since yesterday.

– Bollocks!

📖 What about Aunty Leafy?

– No, can't go back now. Where the fuck is Dartford when we need him?

Where is Dartford? Last seen, three fifteen, outside his house, waving off two friends from the East End who needed help. As he put his key into the front door, a van pulled up at the kerb.

– Dartford Cushion? a man asks, leaning out of window.

Dartford turns, notices two men in the cab. One pulls out a pistol, jumps from the van, grabs Dartford by the arm.

– In!

The guy with the gun slams the rear door and joins Dartford in the back, sitting on cardboard boxes and cans of paint. Roly hears a door bang and looks up from the morning paper. Six metres from his son. He listens, hears nothing more and returns to reading.

From the other end of the van a gun is aimed, a finger primed. The man's face is dark, shaded by the boarded windows, yet he is visible enough for Dartford to make out a withered arm; the right limb shrivelled into tight sleeve and crooked at the wrist. His face shows a lack of tension. He rests the weapon on a knee, casually, like he's fishing.

Dartford considers banging on the side, shouting out, but with the van travelling at speed his efforts would have little effect. The gun offers a more convincing deterrent. The forty-minute drive to woodland is completed without words.

The ground is soft with leaves melded by earlier rain. Surrounding trees patterned with various shades of bark. A rope is pulled around Dartford's neck, his head forced down. Kicked to the ground by the driver of the van, a man with steel-tipped shoes. Dartford deliberately drops after the first contact, to appear weaker, to seek refuge on the forest rug that crackles with his fallen weight. The man with the gun and deformed arm speaks.

– Where's he gone?

– Who?

– Don't fuck me about. Where's he gone?

– Who?

Dartford talks into his jacket, keeping his face away from any assault.

– Don't turn my key. East. You know where he is.

– I haven't seen him for years.

– Not what I've heard, you lying fuck!

No reply.

– Look, pal. We ain't got nothing with you, just let us know where he's gone and everything will be smart. We'll even drop you off home. How about that?

– I haven't seen East for years.

The driver, a big man, steps forward and yanks the rope to raise Dartford's head from the ground to face the interrogator. A momentary glance up before knuckles break teeth. Dartford swallows red.

– Tell me where he is.

– I told you, I haven't seen him for years!

A nod of the head and a knife is drawn. A three-inch blade, slipped up the nostril. There is no chance to compromise, to protest. The steel is pulled through the flesh, slicing apart the nose. Dartford shrieks and his hands move from rope to ripped face.

Questions begin again. Dartford gives nothing away. The two men kick at the body, at the head, tread heels into his cheek as he curls into a heap. The twigs underneath the leaves grate his skin as Dartford writhes to avoid the blows. The rope is pulled taut again; he is dragged towards a tree and the line is looped over a branch. The main man, Withered Arm, pulls at his body with his good limb while driver-man hoists Dartford a foot above the ground. His neck strains. He breathes heavy through bloodied airways.

3

Girls passed out of West's orbit. However, acceptance of his condition did not prevent him from becoming excited by the thought of female flesh, or summer dresses that skimmed curves, or pages of pornography.

He ruled out prostitutes, and refused Dawsey's offer of Rohpynol to aid seduction. But he did begin compiling lists of fellow outsiders, possible desperadoes, who could be seeking the same satisfaction that eluded him; women he had seen shopping, or drunk at bus stops, or sleeping in doorways. Names, descriptions, locations were jotted in secrecy, along with intricate plots and methods of approach, and kept hidden in one of the model boxes inside his bedroom cupboard. Some of the approaches included:

- 📖 I'm lost. Can you help?
- 📖 Lovely day, isn't it?
- 📖 You look gorgeous.
- 📖 Are you married?
- 📖 Can I walk with you?
- 📖 Nice day for it?

West discarded many of the names because of the women's proximity to family or community. Margaret's piece of paper was torn into pieces, reluctantly. Her winking eyes and full breasts. Jocelyn at the Black Horse was always going to be a non-starter despite the encouragement she had shown him once – inviting him under the pub's mistletoe at Christmas, six weeks after Karen.

It was six months before West found a realistic target.

West is in Limehouse, on a cloudy but humid June afternoon, sweating into his shirt. He tries his best to smile at passing women but they force themselves to stare forward, at nothing, conscious of the need to avoid the ugly face creased into some kind of grimace.

West sees her on the other side of the road, walking in the same direction. Sees people smirk as they walk past her, or raise eyebrows. Sees that she doesn't seem to care, waddling proud. She is short but huge, with a nest of jagged peroxide hair. She wears a leather jacket, fishnets and unpolished heels. West observes the legs thumping along, fists clutching supermarket bags. He crosses over and increases his pace to catch up, attempting to snatch glimpses up the jacket where there seems to be no skirt. She struggles to walk, moving from side to side as much as forwards.

West is alongside her and gestures with his hands towards the bags. He grunts sounds, she returns a stare, though retaining her composure behind wide glasses that conceal most of her reddened face. She looks about fifty, and proffers some of her shopping to West. They walk, first in silence, then she asks questions that require nothing more than a nod or shake. The woman is happy to take the initiative. Drivers stare, but both West and the woman are oblivious, now happily engrossed in sharing pavement time.

She is clearly not attractive to the people who pass, even with her bottom half-exposed and the open jacket showing tits swinging freely behind a lace top. Yet she is not afraid to offer herself.

Back at her flat, West dribbles orange squash and they sit at the table so he can scribble conversation. Her jacket has been removed – her breasts are clearly visible through the top. They hang shapeless, slouched on her ribs. West keeps flicking his eyes towards her chest, hoping to make plain his intentions. She knows he is looking and enjoys him savouring her body, despite his deformity.

West is breathless, trying to conceal his clamour as they sit together. The mechanics of seduction, however, elude him, and when the conversation wanes he nervously takes to the door. Not before noting her address and promising to return.

West returns two days later. He walks to Limehouse in tracksuit trousers, which he removes and folds into a bag outside the flat. Underneath he wears a thin pair of shorts that hug his crotch, that clutch his thighs, that he thinks might tempt her.

She notices the shorts as she opens the door, her smiling face flushes upon sighting the bulge. A young man, tall and skinny with a smattering of black hair, appears behind her and invites him into the flat. West panics at his presence, and when the young man is introduced as her son, popped over for quick visit, he swallows relief.

As he walks to the living room West feels vulnerable, his shorts too obvious, and he sits at the table questioning his scheme. The son decides to leave and when West stands up to shake hands he feels exposed once again.

Her clothes and her demeanour have changed. Dressed in cardigan and slacks, she is no longer a temptress. She is a mother drinking tea. Her spiked hair is flat, her legs hidden under loose, opaque nylon. West clutches his bag and gets ready to head for the door. She grabs his arm, asks for five minutes to change.

She returns in a transparent gown. The bulging flesh fully visible, stomach overhanging hairless crotch. Her hair is jagged again, and as she wobbles towards West he stands up. His erection stretches the shorts.

– Do you like to be dominated? she asks.

West shrugs. He does not know what she means.

– Will you be my slave?

📖 Can't we just have sex?

– Oh, West. I'm afraid I've done all that stuff. Boring.

She opens the lower door of a cupboard, moves some magazines, a box of Christmas crackers, pulls out a rubber mask, opens it up in her hands.

– Put that on.

West shakes his head and waves the mask away.

– It's the only way I can do it.

The flat door slams behind him as West leaps down the stairs two at a time.

– You'll never know how hard my life has been! she shouts from behind glass panels.

Back on the street, West slips into his tracksuit trousers for the walk back to Stepney.

Deader Alive

1

– Do you want to die?

Dartford struggles to breathe through battered mouth and nose.

– Do you want to die? If you do, you're going the right way about it.

Dartford thinks of West struggling behind his swellings.

– Last chance. Where is East?

Dartford swallows blood. He twists his neck in the noose to try and relieve the burning hold.

– I . . . ain't . . . seen him.

The man with the withered arm breathes out resignation. He calls to his colleague who produces the gun. Black metal held in light grip, the solid weight bounced in his left hand. He stabs the steel snout into Dartford's forehead.

– Then can you see this?

A pause, someone shuffles impatient feet.

– I . . . haven't . . . seen him.

The crack of the discharge scatters the back of Dartford's head and a flock of birds gathered on skeletal trees. The van engine shatters the aftermath of execution. The rope is let loose and the corpse crumples to the ground.

Another thirty-minute drive away from London, where a contact pushes a fifty note into his overall pocket and opens the gate to the refuse furnace. Grey smoke floats from chimney.

The sky swells, puffed with black and blemished white. Droplets of rain flick against the glass panels, the bags lie on flagstones, darkening with rain. The brothers look out in silence, both absorbed in plotting a solution, an escape. They watch cars and motorcycles go in and out of a garage opposite. East pulls his mouth to one side, West hears an involuntary whimper from his brother.

They move to a café. West sucks up a banana milkshake. East tucks into the all-day breakfast: eggs glazed by spooned oil, bacon laced with uncooked rind, beans spewing from one side, bread smeared in plastic yellow. They are waiting for the streets to sink into darkness.

They step out on to a pavement lined with shops closed away behind steel sheets. A misty shower continues, shrouding the street in haze. The brothers avert their gaze away from each car that fizzes past. The dusk has brought uncertainty and suspicion. Every unknown face and headlight is a conspirator, with full knowledge of Girl, of their departure, eager to phone through their sighting to Control Centre Garner. Their unease exaggerates every shape and shadow.

To the rear of the shops is an open space of broken tarmac and stones, used for deliveries and car parking. Only two cars are left. The brothers stand in the shadows and East pulls a penknife out of his bag and untangles a length of plastic packing wire from a steel bin. West walks to the edge of the building where he is able to observe the open space and the road running alongside. East jogs over to the cars and slides the wire into the car without an alarm.

Inside there is the smell of stranger, of danger. The seat

depressed, the steering wheel greasy from the grip of another. Door panel filled with cassettes and sweet wrappers. East rips out the wires and reconnects, sparking the engine into life. He reverses up, skids the car round, slides to a stop in front of West, who jumps in, and the vehicle bounces over the potholes on to the road.

The brothers face the blazing white forecourt of the garage in silence, there's just the hiss and glow of East's cigarette. East gives instructions that West does not want to carry out. However, he listens, nods, accepts East's desperation.

A small head perches above the cashier desk inside; brown hair greased into quiff, Elvis badge on denim jacket protruding from below the company body-warmer. The boy – he cannot be any older than nineteen – flicks through a magazine, occasionally flicks his eyes up to check the pumps. Three cars then none. Five minutes of reading, then more customers. A silver cross hangs from one ear, he fiddles with it after each turn of the page, after each customer takes their receipt. The brothers sit and wait in silence.

At eleven East leaves the car, balaclava from bag folded in pocket. He steps over a garden wall, snaps off a tree branch roughly the size of a sawn-off shotgun. He pushes the stick into a plastic bag and heads for the garage, crossing the road that gleams black.

Kneeling down by the air and water, East waits for the whirr of the pump to stop and the last cars to drive out. Anticipates some uninterrupted moments. The silence is dense, makes it seem later, like the early hours of the morning. The cold air mixed with adrenalin induces shivering; East feels his blood being pushed about his body. Head throbs under hat, and he licks his dry lips. He can see the stolen car in the cul-de-sac opposite, West a silhouette behind the wheel.

Rolls balaclava over face and leaps to feet. Shoulders the glass door, hurls wire rack of screenwash into the doorway to prevent locking mechanism. The mag falls to the floor, and the boy looks to his side for an exit. No time to run, pointed bag stuck straight into face.

– Gizz the moony! East tries in Glaswegian. – Gizz the moony! Repeated in a hysterical haze, eyes blurring.

The boy hits the till while the stick-in-bag quakes. The boy grabs a handful of notes.

– Poot it in a barg!

The money is pushed into a carrier stamped with logos, which slips out of the boy's grip as he holds it with one hand and fills with the other.

– Where's the fucking rest! In best Cockney.

– It ... It ... It's all on a time lock.

– Fuck.

– Don't shoot.

A car pulls up by the pumps, headlights on. A face looks into the shop where a man in balaclava stands. East snatches the bag and runs. Ten seconds before the alarm blasts. He jumps over the gallon containers, through the floodlighting and into the foggy orange of the street. West screeches the car into the road. East clambers into the back and watches the slippery tarmac disappear beneath them, the beam blazing into corners and reflecting signposts.

East is sweating under the balaclava, the damp wool irritates his scalp. West eases the speed, looking up into the mirror as East mumbles numbers through the hole cut for the mouth. The flickering flesh of tongue, pink against white teeth. Fives. Tens. Twenties. Totalling two hundred and twenty pounds. East delves into his holdall, retrieves a wad of six hundred and fifty. Takes one fifty from the haul to complete Noel's fee, and slips the remainder back into the bottom of the bag.

East always kept control of the cash, and it was invariably cash, for neither brother had a bank account. East, like Lenny before him, chose to keep assets liquid. Both appreciated the freedom of back-pocket finance, the readiness of rubber-banded rolls stuffed into old shoes underneath the bed, a lick of the finger and the notes flipped through. Not that East managed to hold on to many wads; after the bills, the Black Horse, and pocket money for West, whose own money from the Social barely covered the groceries.

Three times a week to the supermarket, the local store on Jamaica Street run by a Bengali family who welcome West with sunny grins. Unlike some of the customers who climb inside their silence and suspicions the moment West walks in, people who did not know West, who did not know the community. People who 'reside in Stepney but do not live here', as East always described them when passing unknown faces in the street.

The smell of peppery spices, cumin and ginger, of cardboard and cans, the awkward balance of wire basket. And the son of the proprietor, Chandi, cheerfully talking away to West, picking him out the freshest carton of milk and wiping dust off a bag of Basmati rice. Joking with West in slapstick, silent comedy. West returning communication with hand and head gestures: the thumbs up, the wiggle of the open hand facing down for uncertainty, the quick pull back of the neck to imply disbelief. This was, for West, the language of social accord, of acceptance, however limited. Those limits were effortlessly exposed when East entered the shop, when East popped in for cigarettes on the way to the Horse. The slapstick and smiles turned to banter and discussion. The development of new flats on Redman's Road, rising prices, the Council's refuse collection, the recently implemented parking scheme, the murder, the closing school.

But East had managed to tuck some funds away. The return from a haul of football strips had remained intact.

– To do something special with, East had said.

📖 A holiday? West had opined.

East shrugged, perhaps.

📖 Some clothes? West continued.

East squinted and waited for an idea to emerge. – I'll need it for something.

2

– Check it if you like, East says.

Noel's smile creases his face like an accordion. The rustle of paper.

Midnight, and the two brothers watch the count. Noel is now dressed in a satin gown; they wear the strained faces of escapees awaiting the next leg of their journey.

– Good lads, you did well. We'd better put the motor round the back for the time being. No discount for that, I'm afraid. Not my thing.

The brothers are introduced to Bobby; he is taking charge from now on. Bobby's head almost hits the chandelier, he's a huge man, who shakes their hands and offers nothing more than a cursory glance. Noel opens his eyes wide and lowers his chin, implies that Bobby knows the plan.

The car is smooth, powerful, and they head out of the gates. East is in the front, a kid beside the giant frame at the wheel. West shuts his eyes and leans on the bags in the back, resting his head on an elbow-propped hand, happy to let the lights of the town flick past as they drive.

East, however, twitches at the silence. He squeezes round to see West asleep, the blast of hot air from the heaters flipping his brother's fringe. East turns to Bobby, notices the blank gaze.

– Are you hot? East asks, referring to the gushing heat that is making him flush, making him panic.

– No, I'm cold, Bobby replies, not breaking his stare.

East blows breath over his face from an extended bottom lip.

Bobby dips into his jacket for cigarettes. He does not offer. East takes one of his own, smoke fills the silence and drifts amid the hostility.

They arrive at a tower block – an obelisk imposing on mauve sky – and enter into the chill of a concrete hallway. The lights on the wall cast a pasty sheen over lift and stairwell. Fifth-floor flat. Bobby fiddles with a set of keys, finally opening the door to 517. The apartment appears stark under a bare bulb. Plain carpet, sofa, table, three chairs, television on a stand in the corner.

– Kitchen to the right, bedroom and bathroom to the left. Don't go out. You got that? I'll be back in the morning. Just don't leave this apartment.

Bobby pulls the door behind him. The brothers stand in the middle of the room, bags at feet, reminded of home by the mass of light dots through the window.

– Apartment? East sneers, then peers into the kitchen. It reeks of dead fruit. He opens the empty fridge, hunts amid the storage to find only sachets of coffee, sugar, whitener; hotel style. The gas is connected and he fills a pan. Sparks the hob and allows blue flames to lick the metal sides.

The bedroom is equally basic: a single quilt, without a

cover, stretched across a double bed, a side table with lamp. West throws down the bags and returns to the main room where East has brought coffee in chipped cups.

– I'd better phone Dartford tomorrow.

West grunts agreement, blowing into his cup, struggling to sip.

– Sorry there's no straws, bro.

West waves away the apology, not looking up from his coffee.

– It seems like we've been away for ever. Can't believe it was only a couple of days ago.

The notebook comes out of the pocket.

📖 Things are going to work out.

– I hope so, Westy.

East pauses, staring into rising steam.

– I haven't even had time to think.

They both look into their drinks.

– Did you see the shape of her body at the bottom of the stairs?

📖 Nasty.

– And now look at me, stuck in some screw-hole.

East pushes his hands through his hair, rubs his red-lined eyes.

– You didn't need to come. You could be at home now, asleep, in your own bed, waking up to a normal day – bit of modelling, a bit of shopping.

📖 I wanted to come.

– You must be fucking mad.

How West always wanted to go with East. When East was a Berserker, West would sit on his bed and watch his brother change into the uniform. Ogle at the jacket that completed the transformation, at the B stamped on its sleeve.

West, aged thirteen, sitting cross-legged on a pillow.

– I'm not going to be long, East said, averting his eyes.

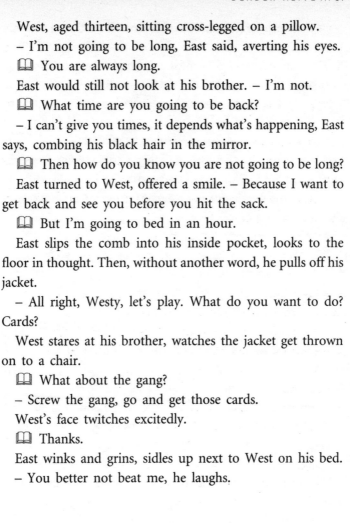 You are always long.

East would still not look at his brother. – I'm not.

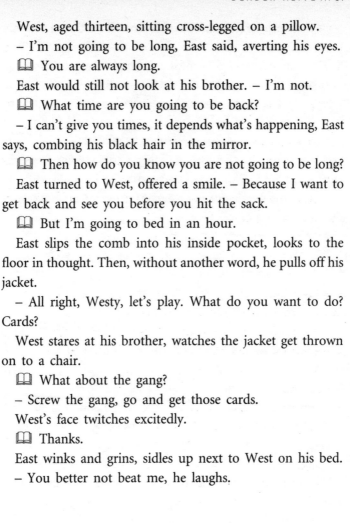 What time are you going to be back?

– I can't give you times, it depends what's happening, East says, combing his black hair in the mirror.

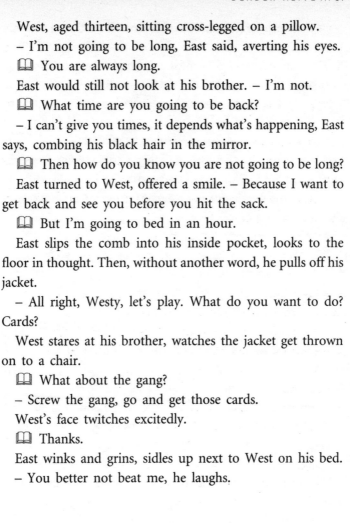 Then how do you know you are not going to be long?

East turned to West, offered a smile. – Because I want to get back and see you before you hit the sack.

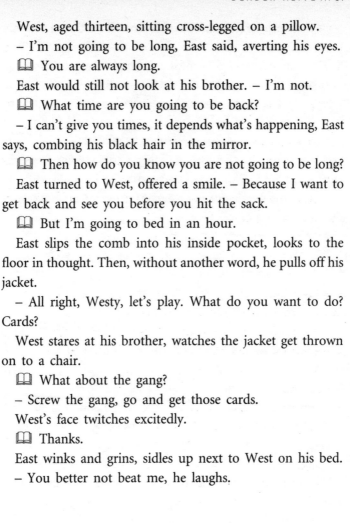 But I'm going to bed in an hour.

East slips the comb into his inside pocket, looks to the floor in thought. Then, without another word, he pulls off his jacket.

– All right, Westy, let's play. What do you want to do? Cards?

West stares at his brother, watches the jacket get thrown on to a chair.

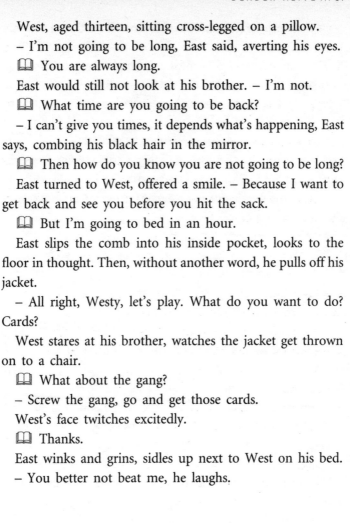 What about the gang?

– Screw the gang, go and get those cards.

West's face twitches excitedly.

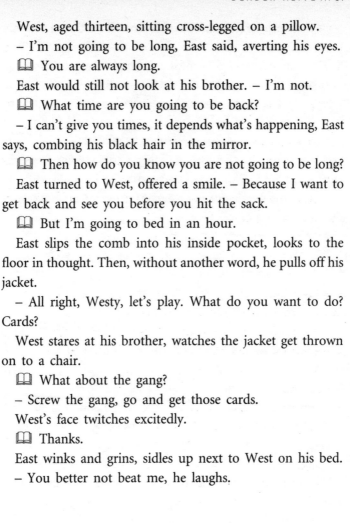 Thanks.

East winks and grins, sidles up next to West on his bed.

– You better not beat me, he laughs.

3

They sleep badly. East spends half the night inhaling cigarettes, sitting up on the bed with his legs pulled into his chest, spewing out smoke as he feels fear gripping him, hot and tight.

West, meanwhile, fights for half the quilt and keeps waking to East's anxious mutterings.

The sun is soon gatecrashing through thin curtains, and both of them lie awake, not acknowledging the other, each wrapped in their portion of duvet.

East is hungry, pesters West to go out and find a shop and return with milkshakes and sandwiches. West is reluctant to leave the flat, to disobey Bobby's instructions, given so clearly. East, therefore, clambers from the bed and pulls on creased jeans, bemoaning his state as he wriggles his feet into damp socks.

– I won't be a tick, he says, strutting from the bedroom to the living room to the front door that explodes shut.

West decides to wash, make tea, sort out a change of clothes. Unlike East, he did not think about bringing sweatshirts or tracksuit trousers, he did not think about the practical aspects of the flight. He loaded his two best shirts, designer jeans, his expensive shoes. For West, the bunk wasn't meant to involve sleeping on floors, in dingy flats, on the back seats of cars driven by giant strangers.

West is sitting at the table, trying to pour tea into his restricted mouth. The saucer is held beneath his jaw to catch the drips, his tongue is lapping behind quashed lips, vainly trying to pull in liquid.

There is a voice outside that sounds close. West goes to the glass and sees two girls below, gesturing to an old man leaning out of next door's flat. West presses the side of his face against the front wall to see the old man calling, now shouting, at the girls who have turned their hands back to stone throwing. At a dog that limps across the enclosed courtyard between the three buildings. The stones bounce off the dog, the girls' faces are alight with thrill, cheering every thud on fur. The old man continues to remonstrate, clearing his throat in between each holler, but the girls wait for the hobbling dog to disappear through a fence before they turn their attentions to the man leaning out of the window.

The girls move nearer to the building, collect hunks of brick from the ground, and exchange words and nods before craning their necks upwards.

The first throw of brick doesn't make it to the fifth floor. West moves from the window into the middle of the room as a precaution. The brick lands harmlessly on the encircling pavement, splintering into rusty shards. The second throw, however, makes more of an impact, blasting through the window of innocent 517, smothering the floor about West's feet with glass.

A third lump is launched.

A young man is leaving the building, pushing the red doors aside for another day of deliveries in the van parked opposite. He pays no attention to the girls until their faces stare panic at him. Their contorted features are dragged into dread by the force of falling brick.

East dawdles in front of the shops, which are organised in a precinct of wide pavement and large bins. A carrier bag strapped around his wrist, he flaps through a newspaper. Folds the paper under his arm, turns it shut and then in half. He recalls the Millwall brick; how during the rematch with the Colts soft paper was transformed into a stone to build revenge.

The Berserkers waited for Tops to return from hospital. He arrived bandaged about his chest, stomach and head. Still barely recognisable beneath the inflammation, his eyes sunk into purple caves.

The Colts revelled in those weeks of victory. They implemented Berserker initiation rites involving branding (a horseshoe on chest) and battering (to see if recruits could be broken), proving that the Berserkers did not have a monopoly on allegiance. They trotted in and out of Stepney looking for action, waiting by stations, shops, playgrounds, to see what had happened to the Berserker nation. Finding nothing, they returned to Bethnal Green without blood.

With the return of Tops came the return of violence.

East spent the morning looking at himself in the mirror: flattening down the black curls in his hair, smoothing out his jeans, pulling up the sleeves on his lightweight jacket, then pulling them down again. Looking from right, from left, then from behind, twisting his jaw on to his shoulder to view.

The east side of London burnt under summer, the brick estates built from molten rock. The raiding party of twelve met on the steps at midday. Wearing Berserker uniform – the jacket, the T-shirt, the jeans – wearing determined scowls that remained intact as they crossed the frontier of the Whitechapel Road and headed north.

Among the twelve, as they walked towards violence, circulated fear, adolescent anger, common purpose. Only Bloke was able to whistle and grin as they turned on to Cambridge Heath Road.

The past weeks had been quiet in the western parts of the Hamlets while Stepney waited for Tops. The police had turned their attention to the Pirates in Bow and the Kool Klan in Poplar who had engaged in a turf war that had already seen one gangster pushed under a Hammersmith and City train and another found headless in Hawgood Street. Daylight in Globe was still a cautious time for weaponry, and so the dozen Berserkers carried newspapers rather than swords and bats.

Tall Randolph, the Colt leader – walked with a stoop, huge knuckles bruised from fights – did not notice the Berserkers as he entered Angelo's. Did not notice them circling, peering at him from the bus stop, the Laundromat, from the edge of an adjacent estate, pushing newspapers into squares, into smaller squares, until the brick was prepared.

Twelve fighters, propelled by a single wave of Bloke's hand, burst into Angelo's with flying arms, reaching over tables, chairs, hurling fists and delivering bricks in a maelstrom of released tension and vengeance. Angelo crouched behind the granite counter and waited for the tumult to pass. East and Bloke dived for Randolph who, in turn, reached for a pizza cutter, just out of grasp, before being engulfed by a black mist of blows. The tall boy fell backwards over a bench, was smothered by Bloke and East and dragged out on to the street.

Randolph was too broken up to scream when Bloke applied the branding fork, prostrate under the stairwell at Blackmore House. Bound with rope and gag, the Colt with his B brand was bundled into the bin room and left with a single Berserker as sentinel while the gang waited for the inevitable counter-attack.

Thirty Colts arrived on cue, galloping into Stepney with sticks, a few brass knuckles, a delusion of strength, and dismissing any risk from police patrols. This was war. They found themselves ambushed on the concrete car park of a Stepney estate by fifty Berserkers who, back on home turf, were able to draw weapons without hesitation. Colts ripped to shreds by spikes, stones in socks, snooker cues, chisels, bats, stumps, hammers, hatchets, ratchets, mallets, chairlegs, razors, steel toecaps, bike chains, bottles.

The police and ambulances arrived ten minutes later to pick up the pieces while the Berserkers slipped away into the ocean of estate.

*

Bobby arrives at the building. He is not surprised to see an ambulance carrying away a young man. He saw the red pool on the pavement, the broken window of 517. He takes a mobile phone from his inside pocket and dials the Garner number.

Bobby spoke to Geezer late last night and he assumes the Garners wasted no time putting their assassin on the case and dumping East from the fifth floor. Bobby would get his kickback, a pleasant salary supplement that he enjoyed when the appropriate occasion arose. Like this time, when a threat and a price from the chasing Garners proved too much to resist.

Noel would not question Bobby on the capture. He would suspect that West's give-away face had been clocked by the east London network, its capillaries threaded into every cul-de-sac and council flat of the lowland tract that stretches from Whitechapel to Westcliff. There are always eyes, coming in from pubs and clubs, pulling shut curtains, or aroused by the growl of an alien car and the voice of unknowns.

Two patrol cars draw up next to Bobby and he switches off the phone before the number connects. Uniformed police are already interviewing witnesses, those standing around on the bright morning who saw the body on the ground. Bobby ignores the officers as they get out of the car and walk to the congregation by the doors, pressed black trousers swishing towards the blood, the crack of quarter-tip crushing loose stone.

East appears behind Bobby, plastic bags of food in hand. He whispers a greeting. Bobby turns about and looks at East with staggered scowl.

– What the fuck are you ...
– It's all right, no one's seen me. What's going on?
– Where's your brother?

– He's still upstairs.

– You hope.

East runs to the lift, bewildered by Bobby's response. West opens the door of 517 and returns to the centre of the room and the table encircled by glistening studs of glass. He spreads his arms to display the damage.

– Let's scurry, says Bobby. – Swift.

He is keen to deliver the brothers to the Garners, not the police.

The brothers grab bags; East questions West about glass, brick, the ambulance below. West waves a postponement and heads out of the door. To the lift whose flickering numbers reveal its advance from the ground floor.

– The Hogs, spits Bobby.

The trio scan for the fire exit and clatter through a single door.

In the car Bobby frets over his next move, his next chance to off-load the cargo. His thoughts flicker over improvised schemes while he drives equally aimlessly.

He stops the car in a lay-by where there is a telephone box next to a bus shelter. An elderly couple stand by the wooden shed and try to disguise their nervousness when the car pulls alongside. Two arms rise simultaneously, a check of watches. Two heads turn to stare down the road for the bus.

Bobby leaves the car, muttering about a phone call. The two brothers sit up in their seats; West is disconcerted by Bobby's demeanour, recognising the doubt in the forehead and scratching fingers. East is conscious of the mobile phone jutting out of Bobby's pocket.

West looks out of the window and notices the old couple. He looks straight ahead through the windscreen, to minimise their discomfort. The man flicks his eyes into the car to assess the situation before quickly looking back to the road.

– Nosy cunt, East says to himself.

Bobby is soon back inside the car, its wheels tear away from the bus stop. Still the couple do not look at each other; not until the car is out of sight. Do not want to admit to being strained by dangerous-looking men.

Bobby winds down his window and leans an elbow on the rim. A cold wind floods into the car. He picks at the radio before settling for something fast and rhythmic. The phone call has given him vitality, release, and he races out of town towards the motorway with a sense of mission.

4

April sun gilds the gravestones etched with forgotten names. The marble slabs look wet, gold letters float upon the film. A sculpted angel welcomes the mourners with outstretched arms, a benevolent face smiling upon every Garner who trudges past.

Black leather has been replaced by viscose, heads are oiled and aftershave masks the stench of loss. Mother Garner in a painted face, below a wide brim. Her eyes bleed, two trails cutting through the foundation on her cheeks. Long, wizened fingers fidget and tear and scratch at the broken skin around her knuckles and wrists, dried blood under polished nails. Father Garner carries the loss on his shoulders, his head pressed towards the floor. The gold necklaces and rings no longer glint like jewellery, but hang dark from his flesh like locks and chains.

A row lined with stones named Garner: Grandfather, Ma, Nanna, Uncle, Chap. The vicar recites as another Garner goes below. This one with stitched stomach and overpowdered face. She was still just a baby to Mother, to Father, to most of the crowd around the trench. The rope strains in scarlet hands and the box thumps against soil. Geezer, standing as stiff as the coffin, stares over the gathering at buildings and clouds beyond. Bloke, chewing gum in a parched mouth, a collection of white spittle in the corners, watches a sparrow rustling among the leaves of a nearby paper birch.

Bloke joins some of the crew from the pub: Tops, Jerome, Jonesy, who in turn join Girl's friends (Katrina, Trudy, Rashika) standing in the dining room around the table of coronation chicken, sliced baguette, potatoes glistening in oil and butter.

The boys avoid mention of East, though all are aware of Garner's intentions. East could not have been expected to stay to protest his innocence in the face of Garner fury, yet his departure can only cast a guilty shadow. The friends remain uncertain, sure of only one thing; that West has been dragged into the mire. A friend of them all, a friend of the Garners – Bloke and Geezer looked out for West, bought him beers, played him at pool. They even tried to pull a few strings to get him a job.

The wake ends early when Mother collapses in the kitchen, her fall broken by multiple hands swooping to catch. Father claps and rubs his hands, spreads his arms towards the door and watches the guests creep away. Leaving behind sons crouching over their prone mother, Sister huddled underneath the dining table, Father pushing shut the front door.

The road is straight and fast with fields on either side. Homemade signposts direct drivers to roadside cafés and country pubs. Bobby turns into a car dealership on the main road, menagerie of assorted motors secured by a chain rope that runs from post to post along its facade. The car bumps along a track, past the main building, to renovated barns against charcoal clouds. Bobby skids the car to a stop, the gentle rustle of stone, and nods towards a Portakabin.

Musty seats and a steel table, windows smeared in mud that's dried hard into swirls and twists. Enough light to see the urgency on Bobby's face and the scattering of pornographic magazines. East wastes no time reaching down for one and flicking through the pages. West wipes the dirt off an amputated car seat and sits down, looking to Bobby who is halfway through the door.

– You've got to wait here. I'll be back.

Bobby waits by the road, the brothers are safely trapped.

5

The magazines are all back on the floor, the brothers are sitting on the seats, imagining the possibilities ahead. Convinced that the next leg of their journey will lead them to a permanent solution: a new home, new way of life. East considers a house with a garden, an idea quickly dismissed when he recalls the £800 fee. Considers a city up north where they would hear his accent and shove a bar stool into his mouth. Considers a new phone number, unconvinced that he could learn a new one after twenty-one years. His stomach growls over the thinking.

– The hunger ... the hunger, East sniggers to West, then remembers the shopping bags stashed on the back seat of the car.

No sign of Bobby as East opens the back door and reaches for the plastic bags. A carton of milk protrudes. The stretch of his arm is interrupted by an electronic purr from mobile phone left on the driver's seat – slipped unwittingly from Bobby's pocket. East twists his arm around the chair to snatch the phone, glancing at the displayed number as he bends up from out of the car. He recognises the eleven digits. He knows the number. It is the number of Girl, of Bloke. Of Garner. East tries to keep calm in the face of the LCD. Edges a finger towards the call button to resolve the coincidence – the mistake?

– Yeah? East grunts, pushing the word out from his chest.

– Is that Bobby? Geezer asks.

– Yeah, East manages to reply, his face pumping with nervous blood.

– Geezer here. I hear you've got them, yeah? That's good, but I don't want another bollock. No fuck-ups. Just keep them there.

In the hut West is on his feet, his left eye wider than ever before, moving his open hands up and down in an effort to calm East who folds his arms, uncrosses them, bites his tongue, rips skin off his lips, then wipes the webbed window to look out, dreading Bobby coming into view leading an assassin dressed in black. *This way, sir.*

– I paid that Berkeley eight hundred fucking notes, argues East.

They try the car; no keys, an immobiliser. East cannot jump an immobiliser. They survey the surrounding hedgerows and trees, freedom barred by a high fence topped with barbed wire.

East returns to the hut to collect a length of greasy pipe.

– If we get split up, we'll rendezvous through Leafy, yeah? West nods.

They see Bobby standing by the road, checking his watch and stretching his arms. East calls out to him and slips out of sight behind the back wall of the garage building. West runs to the car and sinks below the passenger door. East calls out again, and listens for the footfall.

Bobby is angered by their intrusion, longing for the arrival of the van, not wanting to bother with his two human parcels, and so he rushes to return them to silence inside the cabin. He hurries past the back of the building, past East with pipe in hand, who delivers an earthy thud of metal against skull. Bobby falls and his legs twitch, arms shudder, as his body fights to absorb the blow and return to consciousness.

East swoops for the keys, sprints to West and starts the car just as the blue van swings off the main road and on to the track, arriving at the buildings before East can crunch the gearstick into first. The two men in the cab see the long body lying face down in the mud, see the car moving towards them with a huge face in the passenger's seat.

One of the men leaps from the cab, ripping a revolver from his belt, aiming at the revving saloon. The brothers lurch forward, the car speeds into the gap between the van and comatose Bobby. The gun flashes, point-blank rounds split the windscreen and ricochet about the interior, whistling, thumping. East keeps the steering wheel in the direction of the road, arms locked solid before a bullet flies burning along his left bicep.

– They fucking hit me! East shouts as they weave on to the road at forty mph while West helps to control the steering wheel.

The wound does not bleed initially but burns red and black, just below the charred flesh of the Berserker brand. West takes the carton of milk and pours it over the arm, grabbing a shirt from his bag and wrapping it around the bicep. East eases the speed and settles into the order of evenly spaced traffic heading uphill away from the garage.

Away from the flaring barrel. Away from the eight hundred
pounds.

Enter the Exit

1

Accident & Emergency, Oldchurch Hospital, Romford. Even now, when kids play war with live ammo every night, gunshot wounds still take the victim to the front of the queue. A wheelchair races East to injection and observation.

West waits on a moulded chair beside a man clutching a blood-soaked towel over his hand that now has one thumb and two fingers. Behind is an elderly woman pretending to sleep, though, in reality, she's trying to ignore the boiling in her lungs that bubble with every third or fourth breath. West, too, sits with his accident, his emergency, the sound of pipe on Bobby's head, the clump of his collapse.

He knew East could be violent, he knew all about the school fights, the Berserker wars, but he had not seen his brother fighting out of context, fighting his way out of such a scene.

Perhaps West's presence is a hindrance, as the taxi driver suggested. He realises, for the first time, that leaving with East was not so necessary, so courageous, so loyal. He could have stayed in Stepney. The Garners would not have harmed him. He could have stayed.

But, in that moment of decision, when East said 'Go', West did not consider how much he could help or how much he might hinder. He did not consider brotherly devotion. He did not consider how effective he would be in protecting his brother from the Garners, or whether he would be better placed at home, using friends in the pub, in the community, to keep East informed as to the pursuit.

Staring out of the window that morning, tired from little sleep, shaken by the fall and the finger, West did not consider East and his plight. West did not think about anybody else. On that dawn, stained with death and the promise of vengeance, West looked through his brother and saw his own escape.

2

The police arrive at the hospital, prepared to question the bullet-holed boy about his story, about the perpetrators.

West notices the police talking with the nurses at the reception desk, studying his brother's documents. Murmuring into radios with requests for information, for checks. West worries that the Garners have gone to the Law, have laid the blame for Girl's death on East. They have just tried to slug the brothers with handguns; the Law would be no place for the Garners to run. But West disregards the rational. The police keep looking over at him, they keep writing things down in notebooks. He dreads them walking over and taking out handcuffs. West panics at thoughts of custody, of court, of a sentence for being an accessory to murder. Being battered with slopping out buckets by barons on the landing. Jeered at, cursed at, spat at, by regulars inside who would see the face and loathe, would rally together against the freak. And, following the two years with remission for good behaviour, back to Stepney, to ghosts and memories, suffering the eternal sympathy of a community who knew him as Lenny's boy with the big face. Or simply as Poor Old West.

Suddenly, Stepney scares him more than prison. Stepney becomes a nightmare that must not be allowed to continue. West sweats as he waits on the seat, finds himself short of breath and tries to control the trembling hands. Since leaving home he has glimpsed a world in which he can act, in which he plays a part, in which there are choices.

West knows that East can do the police thing, the prison thing, can do whatever, and remembers how he wanted him to stay when their flight began. Wanted him to remain at home in the flat, with matchsticks, with the photographs of Mum and Dad. With people who didn't know why he could not talk, why he tired of listening to the events of their lives, why he wanted to be a Berserker, why he wanted a job, why he changed the buried letter, why he spent time at the cemetery, why he did not enjoy fucking Karen fucking Trimble.

Suddenly, East becomes an irrelevance. The Garners and their guns mean nothing. West looks past them all and to his future. Opportunity beckons, a chance to break out, break away, begin again – with a momentum already created by these few days of running. He has come too far to go back to the shadows. He must not allow the police or his brother to take him back.

East is unfazed by the police busying themselves at the reception desk, he knows that there is nothing they can do. He got a wound – big deal, he'll say nothing. Does he know who did it? He'll say nothing. But he is concerned about West and the discrepant answers he may provide. He wants to get his brother out of the hospital, away from interrogation.

West is allowed past the two officers sitting by the door of East's room. The room is light, feels airy from the slightly open window despite the smell of bandages. East is lying on his back, his arm in a sling. A nurse is by the window with a trolley, busy with needles and bottles. East looks over to West, winks. East's hand reaches out. West takes hold and his brother pulls him close, kissing him on cheek. West is surprised at the gesture; the presence of the kiss hangs in the air.

Communication is difficult with a nurse in the room and two uniforms at the entrance. East flicks his eyes at the nurse and then the door. He pulls West close once more and whispers four words.

– Get out of here.

West looks at East unblinking.

📖 You mean it?

East nods urgently.

📖 What about you?

– Don't worry about me, he whispers. – I'll get it sorted.

📖 You really want me to go?

East nods in the direction of the guards at the door. – You've got to get out of here.

Finding Out

1

East cannot believe that West has totally disappeared. Three hours by the hospital entrance and no sign of brother or car. There's no note in bag, no note slipped into pocket surreptitiously, or left with a nurse. He only meant for his brother to lie low until the Old Bill left, keep out of the way while the questions were being fired. The police went twenty minutes after West, they left without any information. East knew that Noel and Bobby would not go to the Law.

Impatience turns to frustration, to anger. Then anxiety; the fear that West has been caught. Killed in revenge, held as a hostage, tortured with DIY tools, screaming through an already distorted face. The prospect terrifies East, the very image makes his legs shiver. All he can do is wait, hope that his brother will arrive with his face contorted into a smile behind the windscreen. With this image, East curls up on a bench in the hospital foyer and feels the painkillers working inside his skull until the waves of moving thought freeze with sleep.

Having ignored the questions of hospital porters and sympathetic security guards, East opens his eyes at six a.m. and winces at the hurt in his arm. They wanted to keep him under observation, he wanted to go, they wanted to move him from the lobby, he wanted to stay. Now, with dawn barely breaking, a doctor from A & E approaches and expresses concern at the wound, at the night's sleep on the bleached bench. East shrugs and insists that his brother will soon arrive.

Soon after, he gives up the wait in the lobby and changes a fiver at the hospital shop. The phone calls prove futile.

Leafy. – No, he hasn't been here. But I'll certainly keep an eye open. I hope he's all right, are you worried? I'm sure he's fine. Why don't you come over and wait for him here, he may well turn up. You could stay until he does, always plenty of room for you.

Roly. – I don't even see my own boy, let alone yours!

Tops. – Bit hard to talk, Easty. You know the deal. Ain't seen West, got to go, yeah.

East is concerned that the lads who witnessed that last evening will condemn him as guilty. The fight with Girl Garner at eleven that left the pub gawking. Geezer had grabbed East and pushed him into the cigarette machine with a threatening hand about the throat, unwilling to tolerate the public insults to his sister, unwilling to endure taunts of 'Bloater', of 'Fat Jam' that East unleashed despite the crowded bar.

The pub and the community never saw them alone, never saw that there was lust at least. Alone, after feuding all the way to the flat, they would collapse from the fury and laugh at their emotions and have sex amid the refuse of their recyclable relationship.

And the Garners? Have they got his brother? East has got to find out, he cannot bear the visions of West's pain. Or, more horrifying, his death. The thought of that huge head being broken without East to protect him.

East dials 141, then the number of Garner.

– Have you got West, you bastards?

– Wa-hey! says a calm Geezer. – If it isn't Foxy.

– Just fucking tell me, Geezer. You can chase me all you fucking want, but don't take West.

– We want you, Easty. We only want you. But, hey, who knows what may happen, you cunt.

East cannot wait at the hospital indefinitely. It has been almost twenty-four hours and West is not coming back. Romford is too close to home, he has to move. He considers phoning Noel to threaten retribution, but his threats would lack credibility. Dartford is the only contact point and he has disappeared. Probably on the piss, thinks East, with the profit Noel gave him. It suddenly strikes him that Dartford's low profile coincides with the betrayal. Is it a Basildon conspiracy to betray the brothers, to extract cash via Noel before depositing them with the Garners for another pay day? He calls Roly back.

– Tell Dartford he is a fucking wanker. Tell him he's a cheating Judas cunt.

He leaves a more acceptable message with the nurses at reception for West to contact his Aunt Leafy. Although, by this stage, East guesses that West has given up and returned to the flat.

He tries calling home, but the line is dead. A reconnoitre of Blackmore House will be the only way East can reassure himself that West is safe. He feels it is worth the risk to go back home, to undertake a clandestine mission back into the East End.

The rolled up balaclava and unshaven face supply East with some kind of anonymity as he walks from Liverpool Street. He does not want to arrive too near to home, to recognise friends and neighbours standing on the long platforms, walking through the barriers at Stepney Green or White-chapel or Aldgate East or Bow Road.

It is early evening; cloudy, colourless except for the lines of multicoloured traffic pushing and shoving their way home along the High Street. A homeless rabble gathers outside the Salvation Army, in stained suits, clutching plastic carrier bags with split handles, their hands are broken and charred as if roasted over flame. East saunters past – the native boy – with his own bag thrown over the shoulder of his sticky shirt, his trousers creased and greased from the day and night of waiting.

He cuts through some flats and notices a group of Stepney adolescents mingling outside the foodstore on Sidney Street. Familiar faces of the next generation growing up in the shadows. Loose clothes, hair ripped short under caps, hefty training shoes. No longer Berserkers, or Colts, or Bounty Hunters, or Savage Nomads, or East-Side Crew, or Big-Ups, or V-Snakes, or City Breakers, but still affiliated through road boundaries, through familial connections, through friends of friends.

East recognises Jamie Simpson – his mother cleans the Black Horse. Tony Willis – his oldest brother was in East's year at school. Lateef Dale – hiding under hooded top, he boxes at the Boys' Club. East has to avoid the young gamins who swig and survey the streets in the search for ideas and action and reasons to shout. Who usually wait outside the Black Horse, or on the estate, ready to be used as runners, informers, carriers, movers. They would be able to inform on East seen sneaking back on to the patch.

Shifting through the back streets of back streets, East reaches the city farm and settles down beside a wooden stable. He sits on his holdall, rams himself up against slatted panels and spreads his shoes flat on the ground. Stares up at the twelfth floor, at their flat, and awaits a beam to confirm West's presence. Windows dotted over the facing wall of the block are orange, yellow, white, as the residents flick switches and close curtains. The two visible rooms of their flat remain in darkness. East waits.

East struggles to his feet as colour emerges in the muted morning. His arm still burns beneath its bandage, his legs and back are stiff from surveillance. He walks crab-like to the fence and clambers carefully through the posts, his mind gradually returning from the trance of his all-night vigil.

Uncertain as to his next move now that West has disappeared, East is unable to recall any indications, any signs as to his whereabouts that West may have made, and he may have missed. East tries to jog his memory into revealing clues crucial to his brother's departure as he jogs on the empty road away from the Clichy estate. The hollow slap of his sneakers, the clear smell of morning. The air stings East's eyes, which are foggy and strained from constant focus and fitful sleep, his mouth secretes vinegar, his creaky legs running for the first train.

2

It would seem logical to head north, to Manchester, Glasgow, Liverpool, but East cannot contemplate a life among northern vowels and away from the home smoke. His head screams at him to skip town, to hit the trains from King's Cross, from Euston, but he clutches at excuses to avoid hurtling to a distant name. Never been there. Don't speak the lingo. Would get lost. On the brink of escape, East clings to the city and resurfaces at Edgware Road – end of the line – to breathe relieving London miasma and convince himself that there are alternatives. He considers them as he stands on the corner of an unknown street in West London, in anonymity. Never been here, he thinks. Don't know anyone who has ever been here. This might do. At least here he will be able to assimilate with the common accent, a shared knowledge of landmarks – Thames, City, Regent's Park – the binding between the disparate towns and hamlets gathered under the name of London.

He will not venture east, or into Soho, or into the other thoroughfares of the capital. He will phone Leafy once a day and hope that West has returned.

Paddington is bright; it beams a welcome on the refugee who traipses along Star Street, then Sussex Gardens, directed by a *Standard* seller outside Marks and Spencer. Biting into a chocolate bar bought on the Edgware Road, that fills his mouth with brown glue, East searches for a DSS hotel among expensive, white-painted homes with their gold-plated signs, knockers, letter boxes.

The large door, with pock-marked glass, scrapes open and East talks to a Spanish woman behind the serving hatch. The telephone interrupts his enquiries and he slouches on to one foot and waits, pushed up against the wall by guests gabbling in German or Dutch. East doesn't know any foreign languages. The departing group smells of coffee and cannabis.

East's first night in the hotel is not good. Three bunk beds in a room for six, with sheets that smell of cheese. One of the sleeping occupants talks aloud while a guitarist strums tuneless notes in an adjacent room. Into bed at three in the afternoon, sleep falls easily upon East, shattered from the previous night. But his initial slumber is short-lived. He's woken intermittently by shots of agony in his arm, the early evening influx of room-mates, the guitar, the jolts of dreams at one, two, three, four a.m. Disoriented, unable to recall in which place, in which bedroom, he is lying. Occasionally he wakes thinking that the room is a dream, and he folds himself back into sleep, under stiff linen.

The next morning Paddington is cacophonous. Taxis belt along Praed Street over trenches and pits of broken road, roaring diesel over the crowds charging out of the train station, swarming over pavements and crossings. Amid this chaos, East lugs his holdall to the laundrette and throws the contents into a tub. He calls Leafy – she has heard nothing from West – and points her towards hospitals, the police, Missing Persons.

Their phone conversation unsettles Leafy and she dials the numbers the moment East hangs up.

He orders a pint in a pub on the corner opposite the station, stands at the bar in turtleneck and joggers. Enquires about work with some of the locals perched on stools. They mumble an inability to help. They study the sleeve bulging with bandage. They turn to their beer, away from the stranger's chat. East places his empty glass by the taps and leaves to a suspicious grunt from the barman.

The second night is worse. A giant Russian sits naked on the edge of the bottom bunk. East greets him with a slight nod, the Russian jeers back through broken teeth and rubs his balding scalp. Then he stands up and stumbles out to the corridor, crashing the door aside. He returns after fifteen minutes, clutching a fading erection. East stares at the man, prepares himself to translate tension into action, ready to strike fist into face and grab his bag.

With a knife taken from his rucksack, the Russian cuts at the carpet, hacking out squares, circles, shapes. He collapses his huge frame on to the bunk and slices at the wooden posts while the room tries to sleep away the awkward guest. East shuts his eyes to the sound of blade on wood and waits to feel the slightest intrusion on his bunk as the signal to launch the pre-emptive strike. Falls into dreams gradually; the bulb is still bright and the Russian continues to scratch.

By the time East wakes the room is empty, the Russian has gone, and a small South Asian woman is urging East to leave. A vacuum cleaner is dragged in, turned on, and he slides down from the bunk. The cleaner stops the machine and points at the dismembered carpet, yelling at East in broken English. East holds up his hands and shakes his head. Another day in Paddington begins. Out into the strange streets, pavements, people. A bag-woman asks for change, East growls. She shouts back. He goes into a burger bar for breakfast.

He worries about West, a concern that lies heavy inside and pumps panic around his body. East considers the trauma of the escape, the suddenness of it all. From normality to confusion. He could not expect West to endure it all. There was no need for him to bear the burden.

And now, with an unfamiliar reality, what can East do? Wait for word. Get a new life in Paddington and hope time will yield happiness or allow a return to Stepney. Here, six miles from the twelfth-floor flat, in a neighbourhood that must contain its own Tops and Jonesy. Its own Black Horse. Its own Garners. But, unfortunately, it does not contain people East has seen in playgrounds, in short trousers, in agony, in anger, in love, in games, in families, in gangs. That has been replaced by a space he has not grown up in, run in, hidden in, fought in, screwed in. The shop windows have not reflected his twenty-one years from toddler to nipper to snapper to bopper to man.

And East remembers how West could not look at himself.

His arm is feeling better, the bandages continue to soak up the dregs of the wound. East dismisses it as an exaggerated graze and concentrates on finding work. He needs to find employment, earn some cash to get out of the hotel. Picks up a copy of the local rag, a jobs magazine, a pack of gum to chew over the unnerving task of work hunting. He'll seek introverted employment; a job that will keep him off the streets and out of hunters' view.

Driver required. Must be aged 25+ and hold clean licence. Duties will include light lifting and deliveries in the London area. Salary negotiable, depending on age and experience.

East can imagine taking a drop to East London, arriving through the fog of London traffic and unlocking the rear doors before the waiting client recognises a wanted man. The foreman back at the depot checking his watch and cursing the new driver who went to Wapping and didn't return.

Car Valet required. Experience preferred but not essential. Duties will include the internal and external cleaning of vehicles. Uniform and training will be provided by this expanding company.

What would happen if Father Garner rolled into the garage to a brisk salute from the valet team? Recognises the face of killer East under the company cap and returns with his own cleaning squad. Leaving behind blood to be hosed off the forecourt.

Security Officer required for large department store. Must be 21+ and be able to provide suitable references. Good rates of pay.

East envisages the potential. New boy last seen running from shop. The hat, the truncheon, the badge, left as a trail of debris through the door and on the pavement. The other staff watching with disbelief. The other staff unable to understand the significant arrival of Mother Garner and Sister.

East goes to a phone box and calls about night work at an engineering company, C.P. Tools. He talks to the foreman. The job is eight p.m. to six a.m., regular tea breaks, half hour for a sandwich at one. Fixing hinges, punching holes for hinges, dunking hinges in vats of acid, smoothing hinges on coarse belts that rattle round at speed. East accepts for a couple of hundred notes a week. Night work will allow him the camouflage of dusk and the relative seclusion of a self-contained factory. He'll be able to sleep during the day when the world happens, when the sun acts like a spotlight on the hidden. No traversing the city, no mingling with the public, little chance of exposure.

He walks to the job in Lisson Grove, a pocket of working-class Westminster. The neighbourhood reminds East of home more than the grand facades and claustrophobia of the area south of Marylebone Road. There is more width to the streets, less height to the buildings, more desolation about the council flats, the three-storey schools, the basketball court squeezed between blocks.

The factory building is Victorian, built in brick, tiny windows perforating the upper parts of each wall. Graffiti splashes the end facing the street, at the far end is the loading bay, with a platform and an enormous metal door that folds fan-like to one side. There are two floors inside; the ground for hinge storage, packing and loading. The first for offices (deserted at night), and the open-plan work area with benches, machines, vats and a small, glass-walled cubicle in the centre for the shift manager.

Twelve employees leave dusk behind and enter the yellow

light of workhouse. The dozen include the shift manager and the technical supervisor, who wanders the building with spanner and hammer and white overcoat.

East is instructed on the hinge grinder, on ten hours of grinding out the bumps and globules of imperfection on zinc casings. Briefing him, and working alongside him, is Roger. Bespectacled, fifty, he drags along his body, sagging under beige apron. Hair sprouts from ears and nose.

– You take your first shell from the right-hand bin. Check the top. Check the bottom. Then grind.

Both men watch intensely as sparks scatter off the spinning belt.

– Check the top and then check the bottom for smoothness. Then you put the hinge, as carefully as you can, into the left-hand bin.

– Okay, says East, I reckon I can do that without too much trouble.

– I'll show you another, Roger says slowly. – You take your second shell from the right-hand bin. Check the top. Check the bottom. Then grind.

Roger stares at the belt, East glances about the room.

– Check the top and then check the bottom for smoothness. Put it, carefully mind, into the left-hand bin.

– Righty oh, Rodge. I'm pretty sure I've got that.

– Do you want me to show you one more?

The buzz and rattle of the belt drowns out the other sounds in the large room; the shish of white-hot hinges dunked into water, the rat-tat-tat of precision tools puncturing strips of copper, the clump of an industrial staple gun joining alloy plates together. By the vats in the far corner stand two men with Down's syndrome. They're wearing plastic goggles and rubber smocks, licking their lips and enthusiastically plunging and draining, plunging and draining. One of them takes his eye off the bubbling vat for a moment and sees East leaning against the grinding machine. The man in the goggles lifts his rubber-gloved hand and bursts with a smile, eyes disappearing under facial forces. East shows him a thumb, returns the grin, and turns back to work, plunging his own hand into the bin. The wounded arm gives him no trouble.

– Time for a cuppa, mumbles Roger. His left-hand bin is half full next to the meagre covering in East's.

They drink tea from an urn around a vacant work bench. The ten workers, not joined by the manager and supervisor, break into couples to talk, except for Roger who sits in silence alone, and East who sits amid the isolation of his own newcoming.

The men with Down's syndrome hold their cups close to their faces.

Two lads, aged eighteen or so, move their stools together, turning their backs on two old men in their sixties biting into biscuits, and two women, hunched face-to-face over the corner of the table, with cigarettes and sharp elbows. One in her forties, with tiny mouth and fidgety fingers; one in her thirties, with lifeless hair. Both drink from the disposable cups, sitting next to reticent Roger who appears to be melting into his stool, disappearing from East's eye level with each sip.

With the belt spinning and sparks showering, East is able to refine the hinge casing and his life; able to use the time drowned in sparks to consider possibilities, solutions. He has contained his worry for West, reassured by Leafy's involvement, and is now preoccupied with his own predicament. He has a deal with the hotel manager that gives him a bed for seven hours each day. He is quite able to sleep through the Hoovering and the flapping of fresh sheets in nearby rooms.

The first week goes quickly, and at six on Friday the factory floor is soon cleared. Only the two plungers at the vats seem reluctant to leave, finally they rip off goggles to reveal rings on each face. The two of them laugh at the indentations and swagger for their coats, still smiling.

The younger woman, the one with limp hair, is pressed against a mirror by the cloakrooms, digging a finger into her left eye.

– Bugger, she says, rearranging her stance for another prod.

– What's up, need any help? East asks.

– Oh yeah, yeah, that'd be so great of you, she says lazily. – I've got a piece that's really swimming about deep in my eye.

Her drone makes her sound vague and her dank, straight black hair drips over her shoulders. The flowery blouse revealed beneath the apron, and her faded jeans, give her a New Age ambience that East has not encountered before.

East looks into the wide brown eye rolling white and then back to brown. Pokes the end of his little finger into the corner and drags out a speck of silver metal.

– There you go, he says, displaying the rogue lump on his fingertip.

– Oh marvellous. So small yet feels so enormous, you know.

They walk out into thin morning air, her sandals flapping against the pavement.

– I'm Polly, she says, inhaling a huge breath through her nose with eyes closed.

– Yeah, I remembered. I'm East.

– Great name, baby. I'd love to have a great name, you know. Cynthia or Ruth or Ileasha; something that says more than Polly.

– I think Polly's all right.

– Oh, come on now. You know that's not true. Polly's so uncool. Her drawl hangs on to the last syllable, refusing to let it go.

They walk down Penfold Street; the garbage collection has already begun and a lorry rumbles in the middle of the road, troops of luminous vests marching alongside.

– How long have you been working there, then?

– Two years.

– Two years? That's a fair old time. Always been on nights?

– Oh yeah, definitely. It's so much better to have the day free, especially now that summer's coming.

– What about sleep? I bet I'm going to sleep all day.

– Oh, East, how could you! Sleep? That's such a crime. Learn to survive on three hours like I do, baby. Who wants to spend life asleep?

Her eyes are tired, the black borders of mascara accentuate the fatigue. Yet her body is sprightly, her hands twisting and darting in the air as she speaks, as she walks. Slim, as tall as East, she throws her limp hair behind and sticks out her small chest. Her thin, boy-like hips swing sharply, cutting her way along the road. She takes out a packet of cigarettes, offers. East accepts. They smoke their way to Edgware Road, taking a left towards the flyover, towards the Bakerloo line, where Polly descends the steps.

– See you next week, baby, she says loudly, the words bouncing off the concrete walls.

3

East arrives for work fifteen minutes early. As he goes in the entrance, ready to punch the clock, the two young lads turn about startled. The three of them exchange brief words before Larry and Tom head upstairs. East dismisses their lack of welcome as timidity, perhaps they're unnerved that a new boy has arrived on the scene.

– Take it easy, guys, East says.

Roger is setting up the bins, dragging the empty containers into position for East and himself. At eight o'clock, after an hour's silence in the factory following the day shift, the buzzer sounds and machines thump and spin into action. Polly, wearing a purple headband, waves over to East who nods back, hinge firmly pressed against buzzing belt. Clanking the first finished hinge into the bin, East turns to check the time. A long night ahead. The two plungers are goggled up and smiling, licking lips.

Polly comes and sits next to East at the tea break.

– How are you, baby? she asks, oblivious to her staring coffee-mate sitting on her own, fidgeting and smoking.

– Yeah, not bad. A bit knackered. I'm sure I'll get used to it.

Her eyes are still heavy with mascara, but tonight there is blue eyeshadow smeared over each lid. The blue looks incongruous on a woman who, East guesses, is about thirty-five, yet it also seems to suit her prominent features and gaiety.

– Have you ever been to Greece? she suddenly asks.

– No. I've never been abroad.

– What have you been doing with your life? I lived there for five years. It was so good.

– Yeah, I'll bear it in mind, replies East, unsure as to the direction of the conversation.

– You really remind me of someone I knew in Greece. He was Greek, but you are just like him.

– Oh yeah.

– You must love Greek food, yes, am I right?

– What, kebabs and stuff? Yeah, love it.

– Oh, baby, you haven't lived.

There is an aura about Polly as she speaks, drifting in and out of East's orbit. She is tantalising yet bizarre to him, wrapped in seventies' garb but somehow a product of the present. He is fascinated by the charm channelled through her woolliness, and the way she flaunts her teeth and exaggerates her expressions. East rides on her conversations.

Girl Garner would have smashed her teeth out. Girl Garner would have ripped the roots of her hair from the scalp. Girl Garner would have clawed her face to red ribbons. East is certain of that.

Girl had a dislike for anything extravagant, overt, different, despite her taste for gold and red lipstick and short skirts. Girl would have hated Polly's nonchalance, her informality, her abnormality – features which would have set all of the Black Horse locals aflame. But East feels something for Polly. And now, standing on tired legs and smothered in sparks at three in the morning, Polly's strangeness drives him on to the tea breaks, to refresh himself on her vivacity rather than the brew from the limescaled urn.

Curled up on the bunk at the hotel, East imagines Polly naked. Her long, thin bones painted with flesh across collar, chest and pelvic curve. Her fragile neck draped in dark hair. East imagines lying on top of her, then Polly reciting poetry or something – East assumes that poetry is her kind of thing.

Poetry that he has never heard before. He knows Polly would say 'Oh, darling, you haven't lived' in response to his ignorance. But he wouldn't care, and neither would she.

4

East has saved the first two months' money and can now rent a bedsit on Bell Street, a long, thin road that connects the two northbound arteries of the area: Lisson Grove and Edgware Road. The top floor of a four-storey block. Dusty, poky, furnished with an ethnic rug and sagging bed.

He got the room on the same day Leafy heard from West. He wrote to her informing her that he was safe, that he was well, that he did not want East to know where he was staying. He did not want his brother to risk his own safety and come running to the give-away face.

East was satisfied by the knowledge that West was okay, but still wanted an explanation as to his brother's exile.

The nights, the tea breaks, evolved into conventions of seating, of silence, of first and last to arrive, to finish. Polly waited by the urn with tea for East, and a cigarette produced from inside her apron. They talked about things East had never talked about before. Polly would initiate a topic and preach and hypothesise before turning towards him with her slim face twisted on to her shoulder so that the hair is flattened against the head on one side and scattered towards the floor on the other.

– Tell me, baby, what do you think? she'd ask.

She seduced East with her unpredictability, her vagrant mind, the way she fired ideas and insights. She intimidated him, which made his affection for her more frustrating. So unlike the girls of his past: winked at, cornered with a couple of stark introductory lines before into pub, into oblivion, into bed for unprotected and detached sex. No, Polly was different. She was impossible to broach with the offer of lust for she was beyond that simplicity; she was into a world of auras and vibrations, tree songs and city hymns. So East waved from his machine, talked over tea, walked to the station steps, floated in her atmosphere before saying goodbye. Until the next night.

She lives in Kilburn, with a man she rarely mentions, a man she only refers to as 'Poppy'. She mentions, quite randomly, that Poppy sits with her at breakfast, watches television with her, that Poppy once told her the Bakerloo line was so named because it originally linked Baker Street with Waterloo.

She lives in a one-bed flat and does not invite East to visit. That makes him suspect that Poppy is serious.

When East asks her to his bedsit, writing the address on a scrap of paper, she manages to avoid an answer and lets the subject drift, past his expectation.

East waits at the factory door for Polly. It is Friday morning, the end of the Thursday shift. The weekend. Friday and Saturday night free from hinges.

– What are you up to this weekend then, Polly?

– Oh, I don't know. Put on a favourite dress, wait by the window for rain. She laughs. – And you, baby, what are you going to do?

– Well, after sleeping, I was thinking about going to Regent's Park, it's not too far from my pad.

– Oh, what a wonderful park!

– Do you fancy meeting up? Tomorrow or some other time?

– Why do you think they call Sunday Sunday? It can't be because of the sunshine, can it? I think it must be to do with religion. Are you religious, East? Do you believe?

– I suppose so.

They get near to the station steps. East is desperate not to see another weekend approach without some kind of plan, some kind of interaction, away from the bedsit and endless sleep. Curled up in the greasy sheets awaiting Sunday night.

East has spent little time outside of the factory and the Bell Street room. He does not enjoy sitting in the dark for two hours watching movies, does not like books, or television – particularly the fuzzy set that sits on the chair in his flat. He does not like the pubs, full of strangers drinking in cliques. Even the girl who works in the off-licence barely offers a smile when he collects his crate of cans to see him through the week. The tinned lager quenches his loneliness, but tortures him with its after-effects the following day when all that is left is himself, the bedsit and the precariously perched telly.

He does not want Polly to go away from him. The morning breeze is tinged with possibility, distracting him from streets that belong to other people, not him, with strange names over shopfronts, on the sides of vans, on the signposts. Strange numbers on the buses trundling off into exotic boroughs, into oblivion.

– What about the park, Polly?

East does not recognise the strained sound of his own voice.

– If you go to the park, you must walk along by the zoo. The animal noises are amazing.

The last sentence disappears down the steps with Polly. Her words are eaten by her departure as usual, leaving East to walk back to Bell Street alone. He contemplates running down after her, begging her to talk to him, to entertain him with her random thoughts, to sleep on his bed. He thinks of excuses to run after her – he needs to know something about Kilburn, about work. But he stands on the street looking down the staircase and getting in the way of the few people hurrying to work. He jerks forward, then relaxes, as he decides not to descend the steps and chase Polly.

– Fuck this! he spits, spinning round and heading back to Bell Street.

East climbs the stairs to the fourth floor and falls into the smell of dust. He undresses slowly, with barely the strength to pull off trainers, beige jeans, hooded top. There are new clothes in the cupboard, bought after the second week's work. Clothes reserved for social occasions that do not happen. Clothes draped on hangers that chime and clang when East reaches for work gear.

East wakes at eight in the evening, a huge sleep disturbed by regular jolts from images of West, of home, of Girl, and then disorientation, lying awake to the buzz of mopeds, the shudder of lorries, the incessant sirens. The midsummer swells and the days are hot, the sleeping room is doused in unwanted sunlight. Eight fifteen; East crunches the first ring pull of the day, a can from the mini-fridge positioned next to the bed. He is alone, drinking from a tin, miles from the familiar, and yearning for a hippie called Polly.

Hours pass and soon it is midnight. East is sober; he couldn't face more cans tonight. He sits on the bed, in underpants, twisting his brain for ideas as to his brother's location.

Thrust into the room is the sound of the intercom buzzer. It's the first time it has sounded since East's arrival. Harsh and urgent. It buzzes again. East goes to the window, left open for air, and peers over the edge of the wooden sill.

Below there is familiar black hair, a black dress, floating its thin fabric about the figure inside. It is Polly, one hand clutching a bottle. She looks up to the window and sees East leaning over.

– Hi, baby. I've been allowed out. You going to let me in?

Ground Game

1

West's mouth tasted of blackberries, dark and bitter-sweet gulps of saliva, as he drove the car on to the M25 at Junction 29. Decided Northbound, selected the huge blue signs for the M11. Other cars pushed up on his tail, swept past him on the inside lane, drivers seethed behind their executive dashboards. West was hypnotised by the rumble of the road, drowning out the minatory reverberations inside his head. Stepney echoes, home sounds, faded into the thrum of rolling wheels.

'Get out of here', the understatement of saying goodbye to a brother. It had always been East's way to play things down in times of desolation. When Dad died: 'Silly old bastard, striping himself up.' Mum: 'Stupid old udder, losing it like that.'

West, however, had seen him in the aftermath of their parents' deaths, watched him sitting on the sofa for hours, as if absorbed in television but with his gaze focused above the screen towards an empty wall. He watched his brother nurse a cup of tea and allow the phone to ring and ring. He watched East smoke cigarette after cigarette, standing by the window staring into the sky, watched him lie on his bed, humming. Then he saw his brother open the door to Tops who asked 'how are you?'; East replied 'good', grabbed jacket and headed off to pub to begin life again.

West is in Cambridge, shell-shocked from the hospital farewell. East wanted him gone. West read the face, heard the words. East wanted to protect the two of them, was unwilling to drag the innocent brother any further into the mire, into the gunfire of Garner. Releasing West into the world for the first time.

West wanted to go: he had to protect East – recalling the taxi driver's words ('You're a sore thumb.'). He also had to seize the opportunity of freedom for himself.

West now had to fight alone, had to prove himself, refused to go running back to big brother. This was the challenge that West had often dreamed of, had often visualised, while burying his head under the pillow at home. The image of himself dressed in suit, carrying briefcase, marching past trees to the office, leaving behind home, wife, kids, garden, to return at six for a glass of wine and a family meal eaten under warm lights before the News and brandy and bed.

A dream that contrasts to the underpass where West now sits, coiled in a sleeping bag donated by a passer-by. He sleeps in the car at night, rinsing his mouth from a plastic bottle of water, breakfasting on chewy sweets and free tea from the nearby café that occasionally offers him a fry-up that he is unable to eat, accepting a bowl of porridge instead. A slop that he prods into his mouth with a spoon and difficulty. Then joining his crew of homeless under the streets, in the stink of decay, looking up from sacks to rattle plastic cups and lay paper plates beside placards that ask for help.

West, driven to the kerb out of hunger, has nowhere else to turn, is without voice or friend in the middle of a city. And so West wandered, his face growing patches of hair, his presence driving pedestrians to walk on the other side, to give him a wide berth or walk into the nearest shop. He wrote to Leafy, was relieved to hear that East had not been arrested, had not been sent to court and gone to prison.

West wants to write to East, he misses his brother, but he knows that as soon as they made contact their reunion would begin. This cannot happen. It will make it too easy to quit. To go crawling, open-armed. No, West wants to wait for that moment, to earn it by creating a life that will make his brother realise that he is capable. Yet hope becomes harder to maintain when, in the motor at night, West struggles to breathe amid the claustrophobia, resting his enlarged face against sweat-inducing plastic that squeaks with every move-ment. And in the morning when each new day begins with him shivering in the car.

West's fellow homeless sleep in the subway. The car is his one luxury, where he can spend time alone, store spare clothes and his purchases – soap, underwear, a comb, milkshakes – bought by the generosity of the public who stare at West's deformity, the dribbling jaw and swollen lumps, and press a note – not coin, always note – into his hand. This money is his contribution to the group of five who share days in the tunnel, taking it in turns to go to the shops for provisions, for super-strength lagers that West reluctantly pours into his painful mouth. The back teeth are decaying and West is unable to reach them properly with a brush or paste.

The money surprises West, the ease with which a single day can raise thirty or forty pounds. This generosity caught him off guard during his first days roving the city and settling down in parks for the sunshine hours.

*

Sitting on a bench, shabby in his clothes; a man and woman walk past arm in arm, a five pound note flutters on to West's lap. Assuming an accident West picks up the note and runs after the couple. He touches the man on the arm and grunts as best he can – Yoojoffsumsum – as he proffers the note back to the man.

– Get out of it! the man says to West, turning to his companion with a disbelieving gaze.

Again West grunts and pushes the note towards the man.

– Look, you greedy bastard, how much do you want?

West stops and realises that the money is meant for him.

– I don't believe these buggers, says the man to the woman, both now increasing the pace of their steps to get away from the harassing tramp with horrific face.

West wants to apologise. He holds up his hands and then gesticulates for a pen with a writing movement.

– I don't believe this, shouts the man. – The ugly bastard wants a bloody cheque!

It was Cindy, a homeless girl sitting on an opposite bench, who noticed West and introduced herself.

– You could make a fortune, she said. Her clothes hung off her skinny frame, the disarray enhanced by multicoloured beads threaded through her brown hair, crusty at the roots. She walked him to the subway, introduced him to the rest of her coterie, who he has sat alongside ever since. They have shown him the town, shown him short cuts, cheap off-licences, charitable cafés, homeless hang-outs that shocked West with the number of fellow drifters, shown him how to get a P.O. Box number.

They share the cash left over after each day, after the purchase of communal food and drink. Now that the intensity of summer edges closer, the group of five make their way into the centre of town to sit on monuments, and drink. Cindy distributes the occasional haul of pills and dust that the group can regularly afford, that West declines in an attempt to break from the habits of home. And like a Dark Ages festival, the homeless of Cambridge, attired in garish clothes, bangles, blankets, in rustic cloaks and tribal headgear, dance and sing among the ancient colleges and modern tourists, twirling loose bodies and flailing hair in a New Age freedom. West, with his lumpy head and bloated face, stands among them like a masked dignitary. A witch doctor. A chief.

West exchanges letters with Leafy. He likes to hear about East: in Paddington, working nights, living in a bedsit, he seems to be okay though desperate to know where his brother is. And it hurts Leafy not be able to say, to withhold from East the information he desires. Yet she maintains the silence West demands, for she relishes her communication with the brothers. She does not want to jeopardise her pivotal role, to lose the joy of contact and importance, away from the solitude of home, away from Ted staring at Ivy in a frame.

On the streets life crawls along. Like Toby, who shuffles on two stumps for the legs he lost in a motorcycle accident. With Toby's stumps and West's face, the group make good money, – sympathetic fivers, tenners – despite the demands of other homeless gangs to share the invalids.

– You lot make all the fucking money!

– Well, they're our friends, argues Cindy.

– You should distribute some of the fucking cash!

– Find your own friends, argues Cindy.

– You're taking money away from the rest of us. We are all in the shit, you know.

– Fuck you, argues Cindy.

Toby and West listen to the disagreement and shrug. West wrapping himself tighter into sleeping bag, wondering whether the group are really his friends. Toby knows them well and joins in the banter, but West finds himself sitting on the edges, forced out into the middle of the subway so that pedestrians can see him better, led away to the monuments, the vagrant parties, the off-licences where he has to empty his collection of cash for the others to share. They have shown him how to survive, they have kept him safe, they have helped him become part of a community, but friends? He has written barely a handful of notes since he has been with them. A nod, a grunt, a shake, a gesture, has been enough to satisfy the social demands.

In the stationary car he mostly journeys to the future, to a new life. He thinks about East, but even in the most solitary hours of night he does not go back to Stepney. Stepney remains behind him, distant, erased by his desire to make a life, find a job, become something.

The rest of the group want to make money and they lie in the park watching clouds form into continents. Cindy (with her beads and thinness), Toby (with his bobble hat and stumps), Charley (with dreads and big boots) and Will (long and spotty) contemplate putting Cindy on the game.

– Fifty quid a go, urges Will.

– No fucking chance. There's competition out there. Twenty-five at most, says Charley.

– I'm going to need a regular clean up, says Cindy.

– Use the swimming pool on Chandler Street, says Will.

A joint is lit and puffed, passed, poked in the air as Charley makes a point.

– We've got to find somewhere cheap to rent, that is crucial, or we could be spending all the earnings on rooms.

Cindy – Maybe try and get a hotel bed by the hour?

Will – What about starting with West's car?

Charley – Fucking A.

West has not been part of the discussion but now they turn to him, eyes ablaze with expectation, waiting for his consent. West sits on the power, acknowledges its presence, looking from behind the ugliness into faces indifferent to his bumps and swellings. West nods, and the group raises a brief cheer.

2

Charley is big in the Cambridge homeless scene. He speaks with Joey, who is bigger, and who agrees to filter clients in their direction for a modest cut of twenty-five per cent. A fiver.

– Out of respect, says Joey, referring to the minimal charge, as a loss leader, perhaps.

Joey knows the game. He walks the streets of the city in sunglasses, in blue shoes that gleam with freshly smeared spittle and the click of Blakey. He sells bodies, mainly boys, who come to him with square shoulders and unkempt heads and empty bellies.

The five of them wait outside Wheelers – an over-thirties nightspot on the edge of town. They watch the queue file through roped lanes and into the dark hole of the entrance, guarded by four doormen with no hair. Toby shuffles from arm to arm, Will smokes a cigarette, Charley paces up and down the line like an inspecting officer. West crouches beside Toby – they share the stares of the clubbers between them – hoping to see Joey appear from the door with a smile and a client, with whom Cindy must walk to the parked car.

Cindy, sprayed in perfume from the department-store counter, looks different in clothes stolen from town: satin dress, delicate heels. Only the rainbow beads dangling from her hair betray the truth, as does her masculine slouch. She is calm, almost relieved to be helping the group, eager for a clean and respectable gent rather than the types her price will probably attract. This is her chance to succeed, get paid, and accept the admiration of the others.

West is not fazed by her decision, or by standing in the line of drop-outs awaiting the first punter. The streets have taught him to adapt, to shed his prejudices, to make use of the potential available. There can be no sympathy for Cindy because she is so willing.

Toby turns to West, pushing back on the wall and wiping the grit stuck to his palms.

– Have you ever paid for a piece of brass, Westy?

📖 No. Never had enough cash. Ha ha.

– I tell you, when I first lost my legs I thought I would never do it again. I never thought I could let a woman see me naked, see my stumps.

West leans his head to one side, urging continuation.

– That soon went out of the window when I met this girl called Zoe. She knew me from school and I'd always fancied the muff off her. Never gave me a second look then, mind you. But the moment we saw each other again, me without my legs, she was uncontrollable. Had my clothes off within the hour. Un-fucking-believable.

📖 Sounds good!

– It sounds good and was damn good, I can tell you. Fancied me without legs. Weird, I thought at first, then I thought, no, she obviously wanted something more than the normal body.

📖 Or less?

— I bet you've had a few birds chasing after you in your time, what with that face.

Joey pokes his head round the corner of the doorway, waves over to Cindy who totters to the head of the queue and into the entrance. Two minutes later, her face pale despite the make-up, mouth in a nervous grin, she walks from the club with a male arm wrapped about her waist. The man is like a lizard, squirming next to Cindy with tiny eyes and flickering lips. He pulls her close and pecks her on the cheek. Cindy cannot break from the frozen grimace. Toby, Will and West follow from an appropriate distance to ensure no rough stuff, leaving Charley and Joey to prepare more paying guests.

West can see a stretch of white flesh in the back of the car, the man is stripped and his bony shoulders reflect the streetlight. Cindy's beads brush over his back, her nose pressed into the parcel shelf as she thumps herself on to him. Together the bodies rock the car. Cindy's hands reach over the man and press against the window, pink palm-prints like squashed roses. West turns away and stares into the navy blue sky.

3

Monday, Wednesday and Saturday nights are spent outside Wheelers, outside the car, watching Cindy slam the door and strip off. Daytime is spent in the subway; West collecting the most money, occasionally asked questions and offered sympathy but left alone by the time his notebook is out and Toby has said 'He's dumb'.

West is saving the cash, his share of the excess, hiding it under a bush by the car. He is hoping to use it to approach the Garners, to use as a down payment on a forgiveness settlement. A long shot, he admits, and a drop in the ocean the Garners would demand, before they killed East anyhow. The pile is growing as Cindy's prostitution boosts their profits. West is hoarding, Toby drinking, Cindy smoking, Charley gambling, Will stabbing it into his veins.

Cindy is no longer able to jump and dance over the monuments, laugh and tease the tourists. She tokes on numbers and curses at shoppers, dreading another night at Wheelers. Once she leans against West in the subway and West sees the unspoken terror in her eyes, even evident behind cannabis pupils, and he attempts to place a comforting arm around the flimsy shoulders.

– Get off me! she shouts. – Do you want to fuck me or something? Do you want to fuck me as well?

Her legs kick and her elbow thuds into West's ear. Charley arrives to restore calm and West leaves to walk by the river. Looking at the reflections formed on the ripples, daring himself to stand close to the water and catch a glimpse of the man he has become. A face, bloated, waving in liquid. Like he is disappearing. Or laughing.

West does not laugh as time passes in Cambridge. As neglect catches up with the group.

Cindy is ill, rolling in pain that can be forgotten only with dope. She is not working – the car has been impounded by police after tip-offs and surveillance, though Cindy walked free with a caution. Will lies on the concrete with black eyes and pockmarked arms, bleeding from the nose with a smile that says *Fuck you*. West cannot bear to see the group crumbling, killing themselves, with any available money frittered away on destruction. Toby can barely lift his eyes from the lager can, from the lip of a spirit bottle, rolling on to his back to play with his cock in front of the afternoon public. Charley skips in and out of the subway, concentrating on bigger things, not talking to Will, his buddy, who needs help to give up the needle but is too far gone to ask, to know, to care. Charley checks Cindy will be ready for a new batch of work he has arranged, working out of a hostel to the north of the city. She cannot say no, the money is too good, despite the bruises over her body, the discharge, the awful pains in her abdomen.

West's hope for a departure from Cambridge and for the three hundred pounds dissipates at the sight of the broken bodies of the friends who helped him survive this time alone.

With the three hundred pounds rolled into a wad, just like Dad's, like East's, West sets off into the city to find help.

Before he leaves the subway he persuades a passing tourist to take a Polaroid of his sprawled friends, and swaps ten pounds for the print. He takes the picture to the police station, along with a note.

📖 Help needed for my friends. I am willing to pay.

A patrol car is summoned and the duty officer behind the desk escorts West to the waiting vehicle. He grunts directions at the driver and his colleague but they can only mumble vague replies that pretend to understand. They eventually arrive at the subway.

The three of them stand over the human shells whose battered trainers fall off their feet. An ambulance is called while the policemen, on knees beside the bodies, check pulses, try to prise open eyes. The arriving paramedics grimace at the stench of their human load.

Charley arrives as Toby emerges from out of the underpass, slumped on stretcher, trouserless. Cindy and Will are already on their way to hospital.

– Where's Cindy gone? Charley asks.

West points to the ambulance.

One of the policemen turns to Charley. – Did you see the state she was in?

– What? She's meant to be working tonight. You mean to say you've got her taken away?

– Hey, come on now, urges the officer. – Don't you understand, the girl needed help.

But, before the silence signifies the seriousness of the situation, Charley launches at West and pulls him into a headlock while slamming fist into face. The police and a paramedic leap on Charley who is screaming and spitting violence. West is twisting his head from out of the hold, stabbing fingers into the assailant's eyes, tearing at the lids.

4

The police have given West two addresses: an organisation that helps the homeless, and a charity called Face Facts that assists those with facial deformity. West drifts back into the hustle of Cambridge, past the old stone walls of academia, back to the subway to curl up alone. He still carries the cash; the police refused payment. Crumpled blankets, a scarf, sweet wrappers, roach ends, dead matches, two syringes are all that is left of the group.

West fights assaults from thoughts of East, pushing the images away. He writes a letter to Leafy to distract himself, pulling a pen and paper from the holdall that serves as a seat, a pillow, a cupboard.

> I am well. Life is good. Toby, Charley, Cindy all doing fine. Got some work ... hoping to get my own pad soon. The weather has been great ... lots of tourists. Still very different to Stepney. Tell East he can wait a bit longer until I'm sorted ... I know he'll be all right.

West regains optimism, feels the thrill of being free from the past, being free to sit on concrete and contemplate a future. And before he allows concerns for friends, for East, for himself to poison it, he takes out the two addresses and stands, dusting down his jeans, to take the next steps of his journey.

West is not used to seeing others with swelling, scars, disease, burns, blemishes, growths, with no eyes, no noses, with melted skin. West is used to being the only one with deformity. But here, at Face Facts, he becomes part of normality. Fifteen faces turn to the door and attempt smiles from misshapen mouths. A dwarf with albino eyes leads the way to the office. Welcomed by the manager, Neil, who shakes hands and recognises West's extreme form of neurofibromatosis. Neil, who slurs and chews on his own words, speaking from a head that has swollen up around the neck and chin in a series of golf ball-sized lumps, a grotesque ruffle.

Neil is reassuring, almost paternal, with a stilted voice that offers compassion. They sit in the office – a paper-filled desk, framed photographs on the white walls of bizarre faces playing sports, receiving awards, laughing, standing proud in lines, and merged into a victorious embrace with Neil barely visible behind the scrum of celebration. And behind Neil's chair, painted on paper, tacked to wall, the words: BE YOUR BEST.

Neil waits for West's written replies, patiently nodding, encouraging West to explain his situation, noting the bedraggled face, hair, the filthy clothes.

West only mentions the streets. He does not refer to the car, to East, to Stepney. He deals in the present, heartened by the gentle questions and kind attention, scenting a recovery, a refuge. West, aware of the cleanliness about him, is embarrassed as he looks at the brown streaks and patches on his trousers; the scuffed boots, worn to one side of the sole; the subtle drift of street odour: dusted concrete, crushed insects, blood. West has not noticed his decline. The infrequent showers at the pool and the use of public toilets have deluded him into thinking that he is clean. But now, compared to Neil, the sterility of everyday people and places, the truth is stark.

The dwarf shows West to the toilets and the shower. Neil organises a towel, shampoo, razor, clean clothes. West stands in front of the mirror and sees his once half-decent body reduced to skinny white limbs, chest and stomach slumped. He is starved after survival on milkshakes, custard, orange juice, unable to push pasta and potatoes, vegetables and fruit into the blender of home.

West can examine his body in the mirror forcing his stare away from the face, but now in the quiet bathroom, with turmoil from the past weeks behind him, he is urged to look. With Face Facts offering help he feels an unshakeable need to scrutinise what they are helping, in this secure environment with his fellow sufferers. His stare gradually lifts from the torso, to the neck, to the face.

His head appears bigger than before: the right-hand side with its bulges sweeping across his face like an unbalanced headdress. A blinking eye flashes life from a mask stained brown from street living. Patches of hair sprout from chin and cheek.

With the Bic, West scratches at the growth. Metal grates against the frothy crust of soap, wrenching as much as slicing the bristles of the beard.

The shower water, as it did fortnightly at the pool, flows dark to the plug. The lather smells of fruit but tastes chemical as it runs on to his lips. And West smiles behind the waterfall. He wipes away the acid foam with a fresh towel that's been brought in along with an armful of clothes – a selection from various sources, mainly the homeless charity next door.

West joins the other club members in the main room. He's reluctant to introduce himself, partly out of shyness, partly the shock induced by some of the faces. He sits at one of the tables and watches the dwarf and a man with severe scarring play chess.

West does not relate to the blemished heads about him, despite his own disfigurement. His world has been that of small features, thin skulls, clear skin. He is conditioned to a world in which he is the only one who commands dropped jaws and insults. He knew nothing of other blighted lives. Even Toby – drunken Toby, legless Toby – had little to share in the way of common experience, of outcast culture. And now West sits among fifteen faces with fifteen defects, and he has nothing to say, to write. He looks to the door and considers a dash.

The two chess players nod and smile at him before returning their attention to the black and white battle. West runs his finger along the edge of the table, feeling the wood's own scars and imperfections. He stands up and wanders towards a display of leaflets and posters near the entrance porch. Pictures of ugliness, pictures of pain, pictures to stir the public into parting with cash.

A woman comes over and stands alongside West as he casually flicks through a pamphlet, as he reads for the first time of the assistance and opportunities available for the disfigured.

– Hello there, she says. – I know you can't speak, Neil told me, but I still thought I'd come over and say hi.

She tilts her head to the right and offers a hand. West turns, tries to push a smile together, and takes it. He looks into the brightness of her eyes, but it is the wine stain over her right cheek that lures his stare.

– Do you feel better after the shower?

West nods and rubs his hair to draw attention to the fact that it is now clean.

– I used to be on the street. It was a horrible experience. I can understand what you've been through. Finding us is the best thing that could have happened, believe me.

She speaks quietly but her voice is full of emotion.

– Neil is great. He'll sort things out. Just you wait and see.

West notices that she is almost beginning to cry, her lips are sucked inwards to hold the sob. She pats him gently on the arm, making him feel uncomfortable. She is suddenly looking at him through wide eyes, lowered for sympathy, gently nodding and smiling. West grunts gratitude – rerrummffrey, aanyo – yet doesn't want to engage any further with the woman. Another grunt and he has turned back towards the leaflet, surprised at how often he is using the limited sounds he can create to communicate.

Back inside the office, Neil sips coffee; West declines a cup as there's no straw – he does not want to dribble over the new jeans, checked shirt and sports shoes. Neil agrees to house West for a while, during which time, he promises, the charity will have found him a permanent home.

– You see, we're not a homeless charity. All our members have a place to live, most have jobs. But, with a bit of imagination, I reckon we can find you a place.

📖 You mention jobs?

– Well, it's early days, but I've spoken to a few people and as long as you play things our way, I reckon you might be in luck. We've been waiting a long time to do some things and I think you are the missing part.

📖 Plan?

– Don't worry, it's just that you've come just at the right time.

📖 What do you want me to do?

– Pose for a photograph?

📖 I'm no model.

– You'll be perfect.

5

West spends two weeks at Neil's, with his wife Caroline, sensing things have changed. Summer has truly arrived, and each morning is ablaze, burning through the detached house situated in a small village on the outskirts of town, centred on a pond and a green with mock stocks used at village festivals.

For three days at the Face Facts centre West makes coffee and teas, beats other members at pool, mops out toilet and shower room. One day is spent in Cambridge with Neil. To the cinema where they sit in the middle of the auditorium slurping Cokes and spilling the popcorn that West tries to slot into a prised-open mouth. To the dentist – for the first time in ten years, since his mouth closed shut – who can only recommend an antiseptic rinse, or an operation. Then to the photography studio for the agreed picture.

📖 I'm not sure about this.

– West, trust me, you'll be fine. We've got to do this to help you.

📖 Everyone has to do it?

– You'll thank me for it, you'll see.

West feels pressurised. Neil has been so kind to him that it would seem ungrateful not to walk into the frame. He moves slowly.

Under the spotlight, the creases and mounds of his skin reflect the bulb, like a sunlit landscape. The photographer shares whispers with Neil, with Bob, another Face Facts executive who's popped in to watch.

– No face quite like this one, says Bob.

– I've never seen anything like it, the photographer replies, *sotto voce*, but detected by West's experienced ears.

West did not expect the shock on Wednesday morning, the early knock in the middle of a dream. Neil and Caroline falling through the door with a newspaper rustling wide between them, its centre pages gripped by four hands.

– Look, look, it's out, Caroline shouts.

West, struggling to breathe through a sleep-filled mouth, tries to focus on the paper thrown in his face.

A picture of him on page fifteen, in colour – the photo from the studio. A full page. Words below the picture:

DUMB, UGLY (AND HOMELESS)

Can you face the facts? One person in six has some form of facial disfigurement. Can you imagine being the face in the picture? A twenty-year-old deformed by a rare disease, unable to speak, left to sleep on the streets.

At Face Facts we are here to help those whom our own society discards, whom our own society condemns to a life of rejection. We are here to give back self-esteem and pride to those people who, through no fault of their own, have facial disfigurements. Please help with our work.

West ushers Neil and Caroline from his room.

– What do you think? she asks as the door closes.

– We wanted it to be a surprise for you, Neil adds.

West stands behind the wooden panels, clutching the black metal latch and listening to the exclamations from the landing.

– What's the problem? asks Caroline. – Neil's been waiting years to run this campaign.

– Are you coming out? Neil says through the wood.

But West does not want to come out to confront those who chose to turn his face into headline news. Who chose to turn him into a cry for help. He sits back on the bed, cross-legged, and stares at the photo, studying the devastation of his disease, touching the lumps of coarse flesh with his fingers.

By walking into the Centre looking for hope he did not, West thinks, deserve this. And so the holdall is slid from underneath the bed and filled with clothes folded neatly, pressed crisp. A damp flannel is pushed into a shoe. The socks drying on the window sill are stowed for another move.

6

Cambridge is cooking, the midday sun bouncing off the glass and stone of the city. West sweats under his shirt and trousers, under the weight of his bag. Aimless walking, maybe to the station, then train to where? Not to Leafy or East, both of whom may have seen the advert. West is humiliated in his new life, and exposed in his lies to Leafy about a job and a flat. And what if the Garners have seen it? They'll come running to Cambridge to chase the charity victim and rip his ears off with a handsaw, or pull his teeth out and save the dentist a job. Violence would be committed on West out of frustration at their failure to find East.

East, thinks West, is able to make it with or without the Tower Hamlet Apaches, roughnecks, running from revenge with light feet and wide smiles. West himself is incapable of eluding even his own shadow and now he's been betrayed by those who promised to help.

The sun is too high for long silhouettes, and people flash past dressed in the colours of summer: yellows, turquoises, greens, and limbs burnt scarlet. People recognise the advertisement celebrity – the dumb, ugly (and homeless) boy. A middle-aged lady asks him to sign the newspaper. Another old man tries to touch his face, aiming to display cunning and expose the face as a fraud.

Into the subway for a final reminder of his sleeping-bag days, only to find no sign of their camp, which has been swept away by busy feet, the wind, the Council. Into the town to hear a voice call from the other side of the road. It's Toby, perched topless and bronzed on a bench. West crosses the road to accept Toby's strapping arms around his neck, pulling him into a grateful embrace. Off the booze, off the streets in a hostel, saved by West's intervention, he clings to West's shoulders.

Following the hug, West writes briefly about the charity, about the photograph in the newspaper. Toby is alarmed at West's despondency, at his impatience to flee the city. What can Toby do to repay the man with the huge face who saved him from an urban tomb? He knows Cambridge, he knows the possibilities in Cambridge. But before he talks of Cindy and Will and Charley, or offers parochial suggestions, he remembers lying in hospital, with two stumps, being counselled by a priest.

The sterility, the numbness. A bleep of medical engineering continually interrupted the young priest as he spoke, desperate in his attempts to enliven the broken body and mind that lay before him. Toby blamed the car for his chopped body. And the priest blamed himself for not enlivening the crash victim with enough spiritual vim to make him raise a smile, a forgiving blink, and confront the challenge of living with stumps.

On the third day the priest succumbed to Toby's despair and dispensed with his usual lectures about friends, family, future, healing. He tried telling Toby about the pain and fear of his own experiences in the hope of offering some kind of perspective. But this, too, had no effect and so, without wanting to concede defeat to the boy with no legs, he investigated alternative ways of reviving the soul. He mentioned other religions. He spoke of life abroad, of art, of meditation. He cited Shakespeare. He hinted at suicide. Toby did not respond, he lay motionless with closed eyes.

The priest did not surrender. He appeared on the fifth morning and urged Toby to go to Norfolk, to a special camp on the coast, called the Ranch. He brought directions, a name, a train ticket from Nottingham to Kings Lynn to Hunstanton. Pleaded for him to leave the bed and promised him a new start among other castaways, where he need no longer wallow in tragedy. Castaways? Toby did not see himself as a castaway and so he rode the train to Cambridge in a newly acquired wheelchair, and rolled on to the city's streets, cutting off the past, the family, his dejected mother who had never wanted her boy to buy a motorbike.

📖 Why didn't you go there?

– Oh, I've been all right.

📖 What do you mean? Things are bad.

– This is my way of life. I'm not looking for anything else.

📖 Come with me – we'll go together.

– There's no point, West. I'm not escaping, do you see? You are. I'm at home, you're the one running.

📖 But you must want better than this.

– That is exactly it, I don't think I do.

West reads the obdurate grin and leaves Toby with a handshake and twenty pounds slipped on to the begging plate. A note that Toby only notices as West wades into the crowds of shoppers and starers.

– Hey, West, I don't need your money!

West tries to ignore the attention as he walks, though he cannot understand the effect of a single advert. Crowds gather and walk behind him, watching the mammoth head balanced on small neck, watching the boy negotiate kerb-stones, lamp-posts and passers-by, watching the boy feel the agony of exposure.

The heat and the attention is more suffocating than West

can bear, and so he paces fast to a store that has draped garments hanging in the window.

📖 Hide me.

The elderly woman sells him an Arabic hijab that he drapes over his head and body, converting him into an androgynous black mass, free to walk the half-mile to the station where he can evade the glares and rattle towards Norfolk. To his only chance, there's nowhere else to consider now that the newspaper has shrunk the world. To Holme-next-Sea, to Toby's secret sanctuary, to the Ranch.

It Happens

1

– You are so aggressive when you make love, says Polly, rolling on to her side to face East.

– Well, you know, that's just the way it is, East replies.

– What do you mean, that's the way it is?

East reaches for the box of cigarettes on the chair, pulls open the mini-fridge to take a can. Does not offer any further explanation. Content to lie in the sexual aftermath, close to Polly, picking a stray hair from his tongue.

The early hours of the afternoon, different from the old afternoons of empty waiting and empty cans. The roar of an engine along the street below, the open window failing to reduce the humidity. Two naked bodies side by side, a sheet coiled into rope at their feet. East recalls the walks to the station sharing smoke and keeping step, the thin face staring from the metal punch to the grinding belt. Now next to him, revealing the body he suspected: fragile, white, mechanical. The only surprise was the thick bush between her legs and spread over her paunch. Black and bulbous, an Afro that when gently pressed with an open hand fills and tickles the palm.

He does not mention Poppy, perhaps it was his permission that led to the doorstep arrival. He's too satisfied to push Polly away with questions that no longer arouse concern. Now she is there all other matters fade.

Sharing gulps of lager, they confess to feelings. East is taken aback at Polly's insistence that it was lust at first sight; unable to reconcile such a confession with the flitting conversation, the nonchalant grins, the echo of her voice always disappearing down steps to the train home. East is uncertain as to his own emotions, only sure that he felt compelled to be near her, to be stroked by her casual conversation and optimistic manner.

The talking soon dissolves into physical communication, Polly sliding underneath East who fumbles with urgent fingers another penetration.

The nights at work become the prelude to days spent naked in the bedsit, the window showing perfect skies, as they eat out of tins and break open crusty loaves bought warm from the bakery. Polly insists that she is escaping from Kilburn, that she is destined to be in the bedsit with East. He is happy to spend the days wrapped in her nudity, emptying his loneliness into her. Allowing her to spout ideas and effortless reverie.

– I love having pins and needles.

– I love standing up too quickly and feeling all the blood drag through me.

– I dreamt about Africa last night.

– I used to play netball for my school.

  Emptying out her thoughts as questions.

– Have you ever been unconscious?

– Have you seen Venus?

– Do you think I can dance?

The phone calls to Leafy are reduced to weekly.

– Anything from West?

– He says he's fine. He says you don't have to worry.

– Don't worry! My brother's still missing as far as I'm concerned.

– I don't know what to say.

– What about the postmarks?

– Unreadable.

– Send me the letters.

– You won't give me your address.

– People are after me, Aunty. They'll come after you.

– Are they after West?

– No. That's why he should be with me. Can I come and pick up the letters?

– I don't keep them.

– Well do!

– He wants you to be patient.

– Take down this address.

East struggles to maintain self-control, to stop himself from running out to Essex and bullying the facts out of the woman who knows the truth. The woman who knows how much West wants privacy, wants time to be left alone. But she is affected by East's distant voice on the end of the telephone line: alone, desperate and craving his brother, his electronic words are punctuated by the passing crashes and squeals of the inner-city.

East focuses on the bedsit, Polly, shopping, work, and sidelines the fear of Garners, the worry for West. He's intoxicated by the lust and the intensity of Polly's presence, finding out for the first time what it is like to wake in a room with a woman, every day, to the smell of last night's meal, the smell of unwashed clothes, the smell of her crotch. It becomes the smell of security. Briefly.

2

East London has seen the photograph in the advert, has recognised the inflamed head as one of its own. Bloke saw the picture at the family warehouse while awaiting a delivery of watches, he was dumbstruck by the dumb, ugly headline and staring face of West. The brother of a murderer who wants charity in Cambridge, who wants the sympathetic public to send him donations. He will be sent a benefaction from the East End, an assassin to follow the face of Face Facts to his runaway brother. If West and East are holed up in Cambridge they will be found.

Bloke speaks to Father who speaks to Geezer who speaks to the contract man left floundering at a garage in Essex after the double-crossing scheme was exposed by the two fugitives. It's a last chance for the hapless hunter, who's facing his own elimination if he cannot perform a basic tracking operation. He's without his assistant now, too expensive to keep him in the show. But the assassin has got all he needs. He knows the brothers, he knows the charity, knows the address.

The man with the shrivelled limb presses the accelerator and moves the automatic car away from the Poplar kerb. Since the trail went cold he has been facing humiliation at the boozer, facing the ignominy of failing to deliver for the Garners. He delivered Bobby, lying on the earth after East's attack, an extra kick to the head out of frustration. The blood clot on the brain is blamed on the brothers. Not that anyone cares. No police involved; Noel's car filed as a write-off; Bobby's battered skull an accident, now recovering at home without a job, or a word of thanks from the Garners. They're too busy screaming at Withered Arm to get out there and bring back the bastard who threw their Girl down the stairs.

3

For a time, East laughs at and accepts the incessant Polly, with her daily meditation – I'm renewing myself – and her daily coughing fit – I must give up the cigarettes, baby. Relieved, almost elated, to feel human again, to press the flesh of someone in the intimacy of a single room.

Polly, in her Turkish trousers or wavy skirt or jeans or track-suit pants. In her heavy boots or moccasins or plimsolls. In her tasselled top or loose vest or striped T-shirt. With bangles, rings, headbands, dangling earrings. She wears her informality, her irreverence, and drifts in and out of East's reality. More out than in recently, gradually losing the effervescence that so attracted East as he fought his way out of an empty life.

– What's for dinner, baby? she asks.

– Shall we get something from the chippy?

– Oh no, I can't eat, didn't I tell you I have no teeth?

She laughs. East does not.

– Seriously, Polly, what do you want? If you want something, I'm going out now.

– Love is my food. My medication.

The words are followed by a hollow giggle, eyes spinning out of focus.

– I'm going.

– Don't leave me, baby. Stay here with me.

He waits at the foot of the bed, feeling the room drain of energy. And draining of everything that had begun to resemble the familiar, that had begun to produce the sense of home. Leaving behind a stranger's bed, floor, door, clock, chair, fridge, empty cans, clothes – his hanging on the knelling hangers, hers discarded about the room; slumped over the chair, balled up on the windowsill, twisted over the bedstead.

He looks at her sleeping face flattened against the pillow, the unhealthy sheen, the nicotine-stained teeth. The breasts weak and thin, flopping to one side. The black bush, chaotic. East waits for her to snore so he can spend time alone, take a walk on the daylight streets where other girls wander in tight shorts. He returns to the flat to see her face still spread over his bed, the limbs twisted into truculence. She no longer sleeps the boasted three hours.

East needed Polly to break the monotony of killing time on the west side. But what was he waiting for? For a chance to return home? He can never do that. As the two of them share time – in particular, the dangerous, vague spaces between night and day – he remembers the reasons for a lifetime of non-commitment. A life of self-satisfaction that allowed for the casual fling, the quick shafting, the routine of Girl, without having to suffocate beneath another person's limbs, noises, smells. Needs.

Polly is no longer the colourful waft of fresh air that East needed to breathe; she is the clinging humidity of August that envelops and consumes. Lying on his bed when she should be with Poppy or 'whoever-the-fuck' up in Kilburn. That flat to which she occasionally returns, never to stay or to sleep, only to collect clothes, jewellery, lotions.

East has satisfied his need, it is she who needs now. But he cannot help her, knows nothing about her, does not understand a woman who wears flip-flops. He watches the feeble chest rise and fall. A novelty to be forced back into the Christmas cracker.

– Oh baby, I love being here with you.

– What about your flat in Kilburn? You can't just leave that.

– No, no, this is the escape I hoped for.

– What do you mean, escape?

– It's too hard to explain, it really doesn't matter.

– What about this Poppy?

– He made me stay at the flat. He doesn't control me any more. Thanks to you, baby.

– Me?

– You gave me internal strength.

– That's nice for you.

– Poppy doesn't say anything any more when I go back. But I don't want to go back. I don't want him to say something that will trap me again.

– Who is this fucking dude?

They sit in the bedsit, behind closed curtains, sitting on breadcrumbs, and waiting for words to appear. East is close to walking out on her, leaving her on the bed for ever and never going back. But her eyes, so dim, so helpless, grab him and mould him on to the mattress where he waits for the eyes to close and break the spell. He's safe, at least, on Bell Street, even if he is homesick, brother-sick, Polly-sick, and sick of polishing hinges.

– Sometimes I forget how to say things, she says, muttering from the pillow slip.

– It's one of those days, is it? says East wearily, checking the floor for his boots.

– I forget whether I should speak or whether I should not.

– Can I make a suggestion?

– Oh yes, baby, I love your suggestions. You're so suggestive. She grins, flashing a glimpse of the carefree girl disappearing down the steps on Edgware Road.

– Try and get some sleep.

– But I don't want to sleep. I keep hearing Poppy's voice telling me to stay awake.

– Poppy again, is it? East mumbles in resignation.

– I must introduce you to Poppy, it might help.

– Oh yeah, when? East reaches for his boots and pushes his feet deep into the leather.

– I don't know.

East puts on his shirt, fiddles with the buttons, takes a fiver from the small table.

– I just love London. Don't you? Polly suddenly asks from behind a closing face. Folding away for the day.

– I don't know about London, I know about Stepney.

– Oh, but the people, the buildings, the sky, the sky is so different from home.

– Yeah, well, whatever.

– Your accent, too. It's so real, you know. It makes me feel part of London. The voices around you are as important as the smells, the sights, and all those other powerful things. You sound tough.

– Why don't you get some sleep? I'm popping out for a walk.

– Stay with me. Go later.

– Just try and get some sleep, yeah?

What East first thought of as mind-expanding conversation, he has come to realise is nothing more than the shallow talk of depression. Chatter is used to fill the emptiness not as a means to overcome it. Where little lines, sentences, gestures used to make East laugh, feel intrigued or invigorated, the same words now do nothing. Polly is as trapped by her random banter as East is caught by circumstances. 'We must go to France!' no longer sounds like an aspiration or a desire.

The vowels and consonants sink to the floor like bricks, breaking against the confined walls of the bedsit. The 'East, East is a piss artiste' chant now infuriates him and makes him grab for another beer, punching the ring-pull and guzzling froth.

There is no respite at the factory. The joy, East thinks darkly, of being workmates, flatmates and lovers.

Roger: dragging bins, filling bins, dragging bins, checking hinges, dragging bins, filling bins, stopping for tea with a hand wiped on the overall. Sipping and blowing, a blow, a sip, change of hands, sipping, blowing, a sip and back to the bins, dragging, filling, checking.

Wendy: Polly's old tea-drinking partner, sitting with the two old men crunching on stale biscuits. Puffing her way through two cigarettes during the ten minutes. Conversing with the old men via the nod-and-share convention of the biscuit pack. Fidgeting with her hair, her fingers, her transparent lighter.

Tom and Larry: still locked in a covert pact, walking away from the urn to their benches, or to the loading bays downstairs. Never a smile to East or Roger or Polly or Wendy. A word, maybe, to the supervisor, the manager. Let them get on with it, thinks East.

The routines: the endless, empty routines that East cannot abide. The dripping of time, people filling their lives while waiting for nothing. How East does not want to be like them, to have his life moulded into a zinc hinge and dunked and punched and moved from one bin to another with nothing to hope for except the factory buzzer and the urn of rancid tea.

Polly: getting in a fuss over the hole punch that won't fall straight, breaking into tears when the tea goes cold, nothing to say to East as they sit with their plastic cups. Just gazing, not even at East, who wants to be ruthless, wants to be a bastard, but how can he? Life is not so simple any more, he cannot just waltz back to the twelfth, to the Horse.

– What are those marks on your arm?
– You've seen them before.
– I know but I've never wanted to ask.
– Why not?
– I don't know, baby. It just seemed rude.
– That's my gang brand. The sign of my old gang.
– The skin is all shrivelled, it feels like plastic.
– Burnt on, with a fork.
– And these were your friends?
– You bet. It had to be done if you wanted to be in the gang.
– I wouldn't have joined if they did that to me, baby. You must have been very lonely.
– The gang was cool.
– This was in the ... East End?
– Yep.
– What did your parents say?
– Nothing.
– What about teachers?
– Teachers? I was a Berserker, man.

One afternoon, Polly wakes to the bright yellow clouds of dust floating about the room. East is at the foot of the bed, necking a beverage, fag held between two fingers. He's naked, peering through a gap in the curtain that exposes an office block, grey figures moving about its glass panes.
– Have you ever been to the country? Polly asks.
– Yeah, East grunts defensively. – I've been to Clacton.

– No, silly, I mean the real country. Like, say, Devon, where I'm from.

Polly slumps on to her back, throws her arms up on to the wall behind, her breasts riding up her chest. She reminds East of what she could have been.

– No, but I don't reckon I'd get on too good.

– Did you have plenty to do when you were growing up? She flicks out the question and the lighter, edging the shaking fag into flame.

– Sort of, I guess, I don't know. Why, did you have fun growing up?

– Oh boy, fun does not come into my childhood.

– Probably the same for both of us.

They blow voluminous waves of smoke into the sunlit haze.

– It's funny, isn't it, how everyone wants to leave their home? Polly says, now moving on to her front, her buttocks pulled in tight to form a solid lump. – Wants to move away from their childhood.

– I don't think many people want to, do they?

East gets to his feet and pulls apart the frayed curtains, the room expands with the light.

– Why did you come here? he asks.

– It's London, it's where it all happens.

– Are you mucking?

– I guess it's where I thought I should be.

– Guess a-fucking-gain!

– Everyone has to move on.

– For what?

– To be happy, I suppose.

– And you're happy?

– Yes.

– Shit, Polly. You need to go home.

– Why don't you take me to your home then, if it's so much better than here. It's all London, isn't it?

– Only if you take me to your flat.

– Will you stop mentioning that place. Can't you just leave it!

– How can I? You just come to my pad and move right in, barely mentioning this Poppy bloke and your own place.

– I have troubles.

– Don't we all, girl.

– I thought you wanted me here. I thought we needed each other.

– It's not that easy. This pad is only small. You've got your own bloody place.

It hurts East to see Polly's flimsy face cracking, to break the silence on his unhappiness, on her intrusion, but he can sense an opportunity opening up before him. An opportunity that smells of blood, of Polly's destruction. It smells of the end.

– Why are you saying these things, baby? Are you drunk?

– No, but I have to be to put up with you all night and fucking day.

And East winces at his own anger, his own cruelty, watching the pale girl – for that is all she has turned out to be, a girl – disappear behind desolation. At first the eyes fix on East, widening, closing, widening, closing. Then the fingers tear at a bangle.

– Can I make you a cup of tea? is the only thing that Polly can think of to say, head bowed in subservience, happy to be a slave rather than a reject.

– No, Polly. It's time to go.

He says it, he says the words that he imagined would be impossible. The scattered clothes now look desperate; the upturned shoes, tragic.

– Don't send me back to Poppy.

East pulls open the door, shows the landing to the skinny girl. With bursting eyes, shaking and broken, she stands in the middle of the room. Turning her back on the door to face the opposite wall, she hunches her shoulders, climbs inside herself. East nudges her with a slight cough. Polly turns, reinvigorated by the delay, and spits at East. He throws his head to one side to feel her spittle spray his left cheek. She grabs the television, wrenching the set out with cables and plugs trailing, and hurls it at the window. It smashes through the glass, exploding the window and the room with vehemence. The crash landing outside is unheard through the deafening roar of her own demolition.

East cannot maintain the composure that has allowed him to take the conversation to such a conclusion. He leaps at Polly, still standing by the window, and wrestles her towards the door. He twists her head with his arms and shoves her into the landing, to the stairs. And then he smells Girl Garner, he tastes Girl's hair as he spits out Polly's lank strands caught in his mouth. The stairs loom and over the screams and shouts of the two fighting bodies East hears the clunk and thump of Girl tumbling to her death. East sees the heap of Garner on stained concrete. He releases Polly, leaving her clinging to the banister, and heads back into the room, throwing the door shut and pressing himself up against it, breathless, shuddering, smothered in panic.

The glimpse of that evening is like a scream. Pushing the eyes and ears closed, in a refusal to acknowledge the facts of the death. It all happened so quickly. East tries to change the mental subject. She was by the lifts, she'd just phoned home, she ran to the edge, no, stop this!

He waits for the front door to slam. Watches the forlorn frame from the window, inching its way along the Bell Street pavement, shrinking, withering in the severe afternoon sun. Vanishing. And East continues to shake, at the abruptness of the finish, at the alarm of seeing stairs from behind a clutched girl. Polly's clothes still litter the small room, lying dead on the carpet next to ashtrays, cigarette packets, dirty plates. Lying in pieces of broken glass; the glittering, cutting shards of Polly. Taken up, used up, and broken up into pieces.

He's aware of lowering her back into loneliness. To the fridge for refreshment. A fresh crate of lagers stacked in smart, shining aluminium. The red design is flawless. He has another beer to fight the sadness. East wants to turn on the television, to add some sound to the emptiness, but the telly is shattered below, stepped around by the pedestrians all too engrossed in their own affairs to notice the pile of another person's dilemma blocking the path.

East drinks to absent friends, absent brother. He drinks to anonymity: hiding from life itself in the loft on Bell Street. He drinks to money: a pile of notes still unspent from last week's packet. He drinks to the Garners: 'Catch me if you can, you bunch of cockers.' He drinks to his holdall: a faithful servant. He drinks a farewell toast to Girl: an apology, a not-guilty plea, an excuse to forget.

The working hour approaches, but East is too comfortable laid up on the bed with plenty more cans to gulp. Tonight he must drink instead of work, for tomorrow ...? Well, tomorrow will be the same as every other day on the run.

By eleven East prowls the bedsit. Pissing out of the window. Burning sheets with a lighter, watching the flame spread from the black hole with an orange rim. Throwing the chair out of the window and watching it snap in two in the middle of the road. Followed into the air by cups, plates, cutlery, Polly's clothes and shoes, flip-flops. Sitting hunched on the cleared floor, disbelieving that he exists in this bedroom, in this scene. Disbelieving that West is not with him. That there is no home. That he hit Bobby with a length of pipe. That he slept with Polly and that huge bush. That he spends each day grinding hinges with Roger.

– Fuck it, he says, thumping the floor with his heel, ignoring the returned thuds. – Fuck it, he says, as he spreads out on the carpet and lets the booze drag him out of despair and into sleep.

East emerges into morning, aching and distorted, in disarray. Moans when he thinks of Polly. Lifts himself with shaking arms to face the broken window, the empty room, the stench of lager. He wobbles on his feet, scratching his arms and groin, feeling his eyes burning, and strains to see the clock, gone, out of the window. With all the other possessions. Not belongings, just possessions: ashtrays, cans of rice pudding, toothbrush, paste, glasses, forks, frying pan. Left behind are the items that even the intoxicated mind could distinguish as vital. The clothes (most of them recently bought), the documents (stashed in a cardboard folder in a drawer), the holdall (still sturdy, still blue).

East is unsteady on feet that step between the glass seeds spread about the floor. He needs to escape the room, call the factory and apologise for last night's absence, although he can't decide whether he could ever again face the grinding machine, Roger, Polly. Now all so unreal. He slips into heavy boots and stiff jeans to walk on to Bell Street then Lisson Grove or Edgware Road or Church Street, all the names blurred into a single location that East didn't understand or want to understand. Stopping at the front door, at the foot of the stairs that appeared so immense the previous night,

picking up a white envelope posted from Basildon. The
address a desperate scrawl.

Riding Beaches

1

From behind ebony robes West peers through the train window, accompanied by the thrap-thrap-thrap of wheel on track. Tucked into the corner of the carriage, he fumbles under the cloak, caressing fingers and thumbs, feeling the humanity that is his despite the questioning eyebrows, scowls, gestures of others. He's fearless as the train rolls nearer the destination, leaving with every passing field the streets of Cambridge and the humiliation that, West acknowledges, was inflicted without malice or spite, merely without consideration, that exposed him to a judging world.

And West queries all those who have surrounded him in life, have bought him pints and pressed ten pound notes into his reluctant palm. From behind the veil, West's view is dark.

He is concerned about the family graves, probably addled with weeds, grass sprouting into clumps, into shades of brown and yellow. Scorched by the bright summer sun – today its rays are broken only occasionally by clouds, crawling slow and huge. He is concerned that East will be angry at his secrecy and determines that it will not be long before he writes to Leafy and invites his brother to rejoin him.

West travels into the unknown expanse of English countryside. Through the glass he watches a glider swoop and bank beneath the enormous mass of cloud, catching edges of sun then turning into a dim shimmer before sweeping back into white.

West can still see the half-finished Canary Wharf left on the table at home, the matchstick he was to use next. He can still appreciate the delicacy of the next move – then at a crucial stage of the construction – just where the straight sides begin to slope into the pyramid dome. The angle had to be perfect or the scale and accuracy would be undermined.

And the pint in the pub bought by Tops on that final evening at home. The straw was red, definitely red, it kept bobbing out of the glass and trying to leap over the side.

And the kiss from Dartford who must have gone on to betray them, betray East, for who else would have known about Noel? 'Noel's the man,' he'd said. 'Noel's the man.' For what? Taking me and my brother into a hut to await a bullet in the back.

2

The taxi takes West from Hunstanton to Holme-next-Sea, to the Ranch that waits hidden behind lush trees at the end of a desolate track. A wooden gate, ten foot tall, ten feet wide, acts as the barrier. On the top plank, running the length of the gate, are words neatly arranged in shaped tin: KEEP YOUR FACE TO THE SUNSHINE AND YOU CANNOT SEE THE SHADOWS (KELLER).

Through the gaps in the wood West can see a large log cabin surrounded by twenty caravans, they are arranged like one of the campsites he remembers from his youth. He cannot see anyone, though he can hear a dog barking and the sound of a child crying. In the shade of the overhanging trees West waits by the gate, looking into the field steeped in sunlight. He waits for a figure to appear, to see him stranded behind the timber bars, then decides to thump at the gate-post while peering through the holes. Tries a grunt from his newly acquired repertoire – ummumm – and picks up a fallen stick and hits the barrier.

A young woman, tall and thin, crooked about the neck and shoulders, giraffe-like, comes out of the log cabin and approaches West dressed in the black gown, hooded, holding a bag.

– Hi, she says, unhooking the iron latch without hesitation, recognising a refugee, holdall in hand.

West is concerned that she will recognise him from the newspaper. But slowly he pulls back the cloak and the woman momentarily squints before retaining her composure and offering a smile that leads him towards the cabin in the centre of the field bordered by green trees.

– Have you come to stay? she asks.

West nods and attempts another communicating groan.

– I'll take you to Keith.

Keith sits at a trestle table inside the large cabin, scribbling notes on sheets of paper, enveloped in the blended smell of timber and coffee. Tattoos painted on each arm, knuckles thick and stiff holding the pen, hair cropped, fading on the pate. Stubble shades his jaw. He looks at the woman.

– Can't get rid of you today, he laughs.

He takes West's hand in a firm clasp, watches the woman duck through the exit and push the door closed.

The two men sit among tables and chairs, walls embellished with pinboards, charts, timetables. At the other end of the cabin there is a kitchen area, now deserted, with industrial-sized pots on low-burning gas rings, aluminium sinks, rows of white fridge-freezers. This is the dining room and the meeting hall; it is the social centre of the camp, Keith explains.

Keith can see the deformity for himself, can see the cloak and clutched bag. He has seen so many before. Though none with such an affliction. None so obviously in need of help.

📖 I can't speak.

Keith turns to West and moves his hands about, pulling at fingers, turning palm on to palm, flicking the hand to various features on the face. West does not understand. Keith looks at West with surprise.

– I thought you must know BSL, says Keith. – I learnt a few basics from someone who used to be here.

📖 No, sorry, I haven't been taught it. Will it make a difference?

– No, not to stay, of course not. But how the hell have you survived?

📖 Writing.

– What about when there's not time?

📖 Writing. Sorry.

Keith has tanned features, turned craggy from coastal winds and sunburn, and he sits with West in the silence of understanding. Keith recognises West's rejected slouch, the fingers picking at side of chair, the one clear eye seeking respite, desperate for a chance to find sanctuary. The bold handwriting suggests that there is strength within.

📖 Do you read newspapers here?

– No, we like to keep ourselves pretty much to ourselves. We look after each other, the world outside can look after itself.

West's face forms into a faint smile.

In Keith, West sees a man like his brother, with cocky glare, square shoulders. A tough-nut undermined by tenderness that he probably regards as a weakness. Keith, broad and hard, sits at the table in control. Quite happy to let West guess at the bizarre circumstances in which he finds himself. To let West guess about the Ranch, about the man in front of him. They listen to each other's breathing; West's so much louder, the air struggling through trapped tubes.

Then, acknowledging West as a suitable recruit, deduced merely from the silence, from the way West waits in his seat with shy dignity, Keith lets the story climb out of him.

A paratrooper, returned from the Falklands War. He had spent three nights at Carlos Water, waiting to head inland and make contact with the enemy. Waiting three cold days and nights for the logistical command to ensure adequate supply lines for the forthcoming engagements. Three nights thinking about death, about home, about those who would fall beside him. The banter and the endless brews made space to forget. But alone, trying to sleep curled up in a trench hole, feeling the frost solidify on boots and the thump of air-to-sea missiles blowing apart the Royal Navy, he allowed the mind to wander into its darkest corners. Into a realm in which dream, nightmare and reality became merged.

He had spent a further two nights waiting in a sheep pen for the word. For the go-ahead to attack Goose Green, via Sussex Point, for the first taste of live combat in a fledgeling career of training on moors, drinking games, pretending to kill. Commander of the battalion screaming at the Ministry in the dead of night, into a mouthpiece soaked in spit. Furious shouts, waking the troops huddled in the sheep pen and those fortunate enough to have found space in the stable.

Another night spent lying flat in gorse having been betrayed by the media back home in Blighty. Civil servant officials bungling while 2 Para cursed into earth, thumped with adrenalin, wanting to end the terror of the wait. Having to shiver all night from the sleet, hiding under pack and praying for kip.

And then, the following night into war. Running up a hill full of scrub towards machine guns tearing down the platoon, the company, the battalion. Seeing brothers in Airborne coughing blood, clutching shredded limbs, screaming at the jammed SLR, lying motionless in cleaned boots, dog-tags falling over their freezing necks, veins pumping the last drops of British blood on to a slope in the South Atlantic.

Collecting Argies in the morning; young men fallen in twisted shapes, young boys stabbed through the head, unrecognisable piles of gristle, bone and uniform, the result of grenades, of mortar fire. Horror frozen on to the faces of the few found bullet-ridden inside ditches – sudden blast from an automatic saved them from a protracted exit. Still the stench of cordite, of metal, now merged with corpse odour, the mist moving up the hill away from the shore.

The returning servicemen were not ready for Britain, Britain was not ready for them. Changed from the conflict, gongs on chest, broken hearts below. Keith left the Service the moment he stepped on to England. Left behind the buried, the busted, the battered battalion. Stepped into Civvy Street and the inevitable public house brawl that left one man dead and two in hospital and Keith on the run with the broken pool cue still in his hand.

He arrived on the Norfolk coast, seeking help from an old comrade, who got Keith some land at a good price. He sealed it off with barbed wire and driftwood, bought a caravan and set up camp. Lived alone at first, claiming benefit, growing produce, shutting out the memories that still tormented. That was before fellow victims of the war tracked him down and requested refuge. Unable to face the post-combat trauma, unable to face a cramped seat on the Underground, a briefcase full of bullshit, unable to build a family home in suburbia while their fighting brothers lay, wrapped in flags, floating about the Falklands as spectres, drifting back to the UK to cry 'Casevac!' during febrile nights; to appear bloodied and naked in shop windows; to whisper memories whenever it rained, invoking images of those moments spent shocked on the hills behind Port Stanley.

The franchise of the camp was extended once more through word of mouth, select whispers, and the Ranch agreement to consider any broken life that tapped on the wooden gate. Lives like West's, coming up the lane in a black cloud of disguise. West, not defeated by war, but brought to Norfolk by the same processes that pushed the dispossessed, the disheartened, the distraught, to find sanctuary.

3

Driving the car gives Withered Arm a slice of power. Behind the wheel he can perform on an equal basis with the fully armed population. He can shout, gesture, overtake, cut up, harass. The car gives him the opportunity to make an impact – just like working in executions. Deformed arm or not, killing is clout and people give him respect.

But he has worked hard at murder – learning the game from the age of twenty-five, securing jobs in the face of unhealthy competition, stabbing his first victim to death outside a pub in Hackney. The softness of internal tissue, the sticky blood. It was an unprofessional affair from start to finish. No alibi, no gloves, not even a plan, he just wrestled the man outside and slapped the blade into his gut until the suited sack stopped moving. Only avoided the Bill thanks to tight-lipped drinkers and a nervous landlord.

Things did improve; he built up his methods and a personal armoury stored in flats and lock-ups about the Hamlets. Built up a repertoire and a reputation – clients remembered the arm. A combination of good luck, good contacts. And his own personal development skills – Withered Arm uses affirmations and visualisations, mantras and meditation.

Affirmations (such as 'I am the best killer in the world' repeated over and over) convince the mind. Visualisations (imagining every successful aspect of an event beforehand: the smell, the taste, the emotion, the outcome) convince the brain that this mental scene will become reality. Mantras and meditation allow him to clear the head and focus on the positive.

Withered Arm is putting all his skills into popping East.

In the car as it heads into East Anglia Withered Arm chants:

> I will kill East
> I will perform a successful job
> The Garners will love me
> The Garners will make me rich
> The Garners will thank me
> I will be the best killer in the world
> I will never be caught by the Filth
> I will find East
> I will capture East
> I will kill East
> I will kill East

He conjures up new visualisations:

East's eyes folding in on the nose as a round plunges into his forehead.

East on knees pleading for mercy before the trigger is stroked back, feeling solid and pleasant.

East lying face down on a pavement with a gun barrel against his skull, then seeing his body jerking as a bullet is released.

4

Those who have found their way to the Ranch live in caravans that spread out from the log cabin in rings, in ripples. Some families, some couples, some singles, living in a community that's trying to forget the past, a community that survives on the garden produce grown in one corner of the site, on the carpentry shop that manufactures tables, chairs, benches for sale direct to shops or at the camp's market stall in the nearby town of Hunstanton. A community that survives on beachcombing; collecting the jetsam and flotsam washed up on the shoreline behind the camp.

Keith takes West on a tour. First to the sand. West stands on the beach, tasting salt on his lips, squinting from the wind-enhanced sun, surveying the isolation, the vast tract of damp brown leading to the scrolling waves. He swallows his own memories of the coast: the hubbub of Southend, the bitterness of the industrial breeze blowing from the oil refineries and chemical plants of the estuary. But here, at Holme, there is wild grass, sand dunes creating their own waves and trenches, empty swathes of natural coastline. Walking over the marshland that stands between the beach and camp, over clumps of seaweed, mounds of stiff grass, hopping pools and streams, West cannot stop himself from smiling, laughing internally, wanting to run and run to release all the energy bursting inside.

To the vegetable garden, being hoed and watered by a ruddy-faced couple with welcoming grins, with wellington boots. Rows of bamboo in bunches, like tepee frames, green netting stretched over lines of raised soil, thick bushes of gooseberry, raspberry, and blackberry. The couple straighten their stances when Keith arrives. There are no hostile glances at West's face.

To the carpentry shop that stands at the back of the camp, by the gate to the marshland and the beach. West is awestruck at the tools, the equipment, at the quality of the products ready for market. The unique scent of dust, varnish, work aprons drenched in chippings and sweat and spilt tea. He watches a woman gliding the plane over a length of hardwood, a man sliding a saw through willing pitch pine. West does not want to leave the thip-thip and griff-griff of the workshop, he is eager to stroke the planks of wood that are stored in heaps awaiting sculpting. He is keen to press inquisitive fingers against the blades of chisel, file, handsaw, knife.

📖 Can I work in here?

– If you think you can handle it. Had any experience with timber?

📖 I'm a modeller. Used to using my hands.

– Maybe we'll make a chippy of you.

Keith can see the eyes changing, can see the expectancy flashing out of the clearer side of the face.

– I hope you're not just saying that to be near Meredith over there?

At which point, the girl who is planing looks up and flicks her head backwards with pretend exasperation.

West waves his hands and groans a laugh. The spontaneous chuckle is eaten up by the similarity between the girl and

Cindy. It is a mild comparison but one that leaves West silent and chilled, despite the heat. A reminder of the past that must now be pushed aside, boxed away in darkness.

Meals are taken communally in the cabin, with trays, filing past the two cooks as they slide food on full plates. Mashed swede glazed with melted margarine, whole carrots, potatoes leaking white water, shredded chicken mixed in garlic and paprika sauce. Sitting at the tables, without a system, joining fellow residents for conversation and camaraderie and, at the evening meal, for coffee and cheese. Staying in the building late while oil lamps flicker above heads.

Then to the bathrooms, to spit in sinks, to flush toilets, to shower, to make one's way back to the caravan and lie on the soft mattress looking at the vinyl ceiling and trying to remember what to forget and what to retain. Emptying the mind of what Keith refers to as 'our black tails' – such things are put behind. Though West gleans from Keith's Falklands story that the double meaning is deliberate. Tales that cling behind, occasionally grabbed and examined before being tossed back out of sight.

West's caravan-mate is Conrad, and it is Conrad who shows him about the carpentry shop. He introduces West to the timber store, the tools, the paint and varnish section, the driftwood recycling area where wood is stripped and planed down to its workable element. He points and demonstrates with the same happy grin – laughter lines ingrained, white teeth. A handsome face on a small frame: long shorts and short-sleeved shirt, the head wind-blown from an earlier scouring of the beach, the short hair pushed into a point.

– We a good family here, you know. With the wood, with beach.

Conrad talks in disjointed, heavily accented English, with strong use of the tongue and the top of the mouth. Like a Russian spy from the television, considers West.

West pulls on an apron, ties the string snugly across his stomach, collects a plane and lengths of driftwood. He takes them to the bench in a corner by the door. Fastens the strips into the vice and begins skimming the blade over the surface, shredding away the rough. Meredith walks into the hut, stops for a second at West's bench to offer an approving smile and nod as she watches him throw the plane back and forth.

– You're a natural, she says warmly.

West does not look up. He replies with just a humble flick of the head and a reddening face, embarrassed by the compliment, never before has he felt so praised. He tucks in his elbows, realigns his feet, tightens his grip and continues to lunge and retreat, lunge and retreat.

Keith has gone through the forms that West completed as part of his camp enlistment. Name, parents' names, date of birth, National Insurance number, all the information voluntarily collated and stored in confidential files. With the dossier, Keith has organised appointments with dentist and doctor, has arranged enrolment at the local adult college for sign-language classes.

West is driven into town in the Ranch's ageing pick-up, disintegrating red with rusted lettering on the side panels. Keith drives, slamming the gearstick, exuding the smell of stale tobacco and suntan, wearing a vest that reveals muscular arms. West rests his arm on the open window, wipes the wing mirror.

Keith was with West last night in the caravan, demonstrating the basic moves of sign language: the wide circles drawn in the air with open hands, the karate chops, the finger pointing to palm, to ear, to eye, to mouth, to other digits. West knows the power of the pointed finger.

Keith now talks, West listens, peppering the lecture with nods, groans, stares displaying interest. Keith drives close to the cars in front, flashing headlights and veering into the middle of the road to demonstrate intent to overtake. He mutters obscenities, then shouts them, indifferent to West who pretends not to notice by faking interest in every house, hedge and passing lamp-post. The truck lurches into each corner while the breaking morning melts through the thin veil of cloud.

– Wanker! Keith yells at the car ahead.

The chair glides backwards and the dentist rubs her jaw and puzzles over the minute entrance to the mouth, over the lips pushed to one side and into a beak of wet flesh. The mirror on a stem is edged through the orifice without space for the reflection to be studied. The spotlight is trained in various positions but proper investigation of the mouth is impossible. They numb the cheek and attempt a forced opening with a dental clamp, hiding their eyes from their patient's forehead ruffled in pain. Still the mouth will not allow invasion. The dentist's options are stark: suffer the pain or allow an orthodontist to slice open the mandible.

The doctor, standing tall over West lying on the couch, and Keith, who peers coldly at the distorted lumps exaggerated by the torch, agree that the only option is immediate surgery to open up the cheek and deal with the teeth problem, then possibly attempt some kind of facial realignment. Perhaps the removal of excess growth followed by repair through plastic surgery. A two- to three-year project, quite straightforward. The doctor is amazed that the boy has never been seen by a specialist. He arranges an appointment with a consultant.

📖 We didn't use doctors back home.

– We're not in the Dark Ages now, you know.

West knows.

The teacher is called Mary, her grey hair rising up into a wave crashing over the brow of her head, tied into solidity by a green band. Her face pale, framed around the tight nose and blue eyes that question her sixty years. Immaculate in soft dress at the front of the class of seven.

– You've made the bravest step by walking through the door, she announces, pushing her hands towards the seated students. – This is only the first session, so we'll use it as a chance to get to know each other and introduce some of the history and basics of British Sign Language.

She moves from behind the desk to perch serenely on a vacant table in front of West. She speaks about dumbness, about deafness, about the development of sign. The routine runs fresh, original, albeit spoken for the hundredth time.

Her voice is like a collage, each word is spoken with different sound. West thinks about the forthcoming operations and the possibility of speech, maybe some day. And he decides that he would learn to speak like Mary, with the warmth and clarity that subdued the first-meeting nerves and reassured the gathered group.

At break time, when the group wanders towards the coffee machine, not one member of the class pays unnecessary attention to West sucking from a straw. When they speak to him, they look at his eye. One of the group, Peter, shouts each word, slowly, distortedly, as he talks.

– Have ... I ... seen you ... in ... the newspaper?

West notices the hearing aid slotted behind the ear and

Peter's already heavy reliance upon gestures – he flips his hands and head about as if swimming, badly.

The rest of the group look to West after hearing the question.

📖 Not me.

The faces bury back into polystyrene cups.

5

Beachcombing in the morning is a thrill for West, seeing the thumping crests of waves ironing the coast, the white bubbles skating on the surf. The wind, carrying particles of shell and sand, blowing open the light jackets, depositing the sea into hair. West watches his feet leaving prints in the beach, watches them getting swept away by the ocean.

Twenty figures edge along the deserted landscape in a straight line. Communication is hampered by the morning gale buffeting the ears. West turns his open mouth into the wind to offer relief to the aching teeth. The rank moves forward, heads bent over. Seeking wreckage, waste.

The camp had retrieved many interesting finds: a crate of mahogany; a dinghy with the outboard motor still attached; a corpse; ancient coins (once a week they use the metal detector); a working clock that chimed midnight the moment Meredith bent to recover it; barrels of various chemicals (left unopened); dead animals, including a cow and a llama; a canteen of cutlery; a sack of bones; a bin liner of fancy-dress costumes; thirty bottles with messages that were thrown back to continue their search for a welcoming stranger. West wondered why the camp did not respond to the letters.

West picks up a life jacket, a few chunks of wood that are hurled into communal piles to be collected later, a natural sponge, and a number of coloured shells that Meredith will transform into jewellery or, depending on size, artefacts such as lamps, boxes, picture frames, pots. The camp is adept at using its natural resources, at devising products based on the coastal debris. The carpentry shop, which began with the mahogany find, continues with the sodden wood harvested from the beach and processed into timber.

West helps carry wood back to the workshop with Conrad. The uplift West receives from entering the cabin full of shavings and saws prepares him for the day ahead – the visit to the hospital for his first appointment with a surgeon. In the afternoon he can pull on an apron, fondle timber and begin to create.

Breakfast for West is scrambled egg; weak yellow, dribbling off the spoon. Breakfast for the others is grilled sausages in an ebony crust. Rashers of bacon shrivelled by heat and oil. Tomatoes, fried in butter with ground pepper, cut in two so that the blackened skin holds, like a bowl, bubbling flesh and juice. Toast, tanned under gas with glinting streaks of soya spread.

West watches the woman who looks like a giraffe drooped over the serving tables, a shapeless body. He looks at the eating tables about him, back to the giraffe, and wonders why they are all here. How they ended up in Holme. With Keith and his wartime horrors.

– Dear oh dear, the consultant says, with a shake of the head and unintentional disgust. – Quite severe, quite severe.

The consultant talks to himself, resting his arms on his hips and asking West to say 'ah'. The balding head with its smatter of wisps, the blotchy skin. The consultant's plainness hides behind the authority with which he places his hands on West's face and prods and twists, grapples and grabs.

– You say your teeth are causing you constant pain?

West agrees through a face full of palms and fingers. – Aaraahum.

– We are going to have to extend the mouth cavity, he explains. – Perhaps graft some kind of alternative to lips. You need a mouth, old chap.

Another mumbled agreement.

– Very silly of you, not getting this seen to before it became so developed.

West remains silent, unwilling to agree to an insult of his parents, of himself. We did not know any better, he wants to say, beginning to imagine words and shaped mouth and useful tongue. We did our best.

– There is so much excess tissue. We can remove most of this.

West does not know what to think, the thoughts curls up and elude him as he considers his face being stripped to thinness and the mouth sipping from a glass. He imagines staring at a mirror and seeing a different person, seeing the head pruned and sculpted, moulded into a narrow face. Hypnotised by the mirror, leaning forward to kiss the reflection and, probably, breaking into emotional release for a lifetime of hurt finally amputated. Leaving just the real West he always knew was there behind the swollen curtain.

Keith waits patiently in the pick-up, blurting the horn when West eventually appears from the double-doors of the clinic. Keith swerves the vehicle past nurses walking in the car park – their arms folded, little hats balanced on heads – the van coughs smoke as it rolls on to the main road.

– All right, then? Keith asks, waiting for West to perform a few quick nods in succession.

– Fancy a swifty?

West's face creases agreement.

At the pub the men sit on the benches in the garden and absorb Norfolk, listening to the beauty. Both bodies are alight in the afternoon sun.

📖 The doc thinks he might be able to get rid of some of the extra skin.

– Sounds good. Might be able to see what you really look like under there.

📖 I'll probably look like my brother.

– Oh yeah, got a brother, have you?

📖 His name is East.

– Cor, your parents certainly went in for the old compass stuff.

Keith goes to the bar, disappearing into dark, fetching another two drinks. West sucks the last drops of his pint, spinning the straw about the bottom of the glass. Hoovering, he calls it. Keith returns, beer spilling over his hands. He licks off the juice.

– How's the sign stuff going?

📖 Only just started really. I'm a bit nervous because I've got to demonstrate the first half of the alphabet tomorrow.

– What have they got you doing the teacher's job for?

📖 No, we all take it in turns to do something up front.

– You'll be all right.

📖 I've never done anything like it before.

– Do you want me to come, sit at the back, give you some support?

📖 That's good of you, but I don't think Mary'd allow it.

– Mary, eh? Bit of crumpet, is she?

📖 She's sixty.

– Forget it.

6

Mary appears to glow in the classroom, holding students' hands as she pushes and presses them into the shapes and positions of gestured speech. West and Peter are the only members of the group learning to give themselves a voice, to break out of silence. For the remainder it is a teaching course, or a chance to learn the language of silence for the sake of a deaf friend or relation. And for this reason the other students take time to learn with West and Peter, ensuring that they are acquiring the methods and the ideas. However, the class need not concern themselves with West, for he is ahead of them and picking up each new movement with the same dexterity with which he picked up the wood-plane.

Preparing to demonstrate to the class, West feels his stomach fill with acid, feels his mouth stiffen and his vision cloud with a nervous haze. The class watch him walk to the front, watch Mary sit in his seat and fiddle awkwardly with his neatly piled set of books. The swollen face swallows, struggling to push tongue forward and wave of saliva back. He focuses on Mary who blinks gently, giving West the freedom, the comfort, to perform in his own time. West reads the face.

A – index finger of right hand pressed against thumb of left

B – fingers and thumb of each hand curled into circle, pressed together like invisible binoculars

C – right hand formed into semicircle

D . . . E . . . G – fists placed one on top of the other, and so on, confidently to:

M – three fingers spread onto left palm.

The class clap and West takes a deliberately dramatic bow, hands sweeping wide, face crumpled into pleasure. Feeling the success, the breeze from applause, accepting the congrat-ulations of people who see his face, see his difference, yet continue to confer achievement upon him. He has never felt the joy before. There was the examination success at school, but such success came in secret. Red numbers at the bottom of the page, closed inside the book or concealed inside envelope marked Confidential. Never a public cheer, an admiring audience, nodding acknowledgement. People slap-ping palms for him. He wishes Mum and Dad and East could see him.

At the end of the lesson Mary and West sit together with coffee and swap signs and written notes. Mary with powder and muted lipstick softening the ageing lines and creased lips, with speedwell eyes and the endearing habit of flicking her gaze to the floor. Her long fingers carry sleek gold rings. She wears a loose skirt, blouse, sandals.

Keith waits outside by the van.

West does not see her sixty years, does not see her as teacher. She sits with her knees pressed together, her hands embracing the cup, her eyes flicking to West and then to the tiles. They communicate with a mixture of slow BSL, improvised motions and West's notepad.

BSL is still easier for West to watch and understand than perform. He admires the grace in Mary's movements as she probes West for details of his life locked away behind the dumbness and distortion, as she takes patient and tentative steps into West's psyche. Each of Mary's carefully formed signs directs West towards another door for him to enter and explore.

- How did you get on at school?
- Did your brother help you?
- When was the last time you spoke words?
- Did you want to hide from the world?

West replies with large words written neatly on the page and, at times, with the groping, awkward fingers of a novice signer, feeling his way.

Mary dabs her dry lips with her tongue, pushes loose, long hairs out of her eyes and mouth and waits for West to complete his responses. She is willing to watch and encourage him as he ponders the questions, contemplates the best way to reply. With an honesty usually suppressed by the informality of the occasion, of other people, at the Black Horse, or on the streets, or supping lagers on the bench with Keith, West revels in the opportunity to speak the truth.

7

Having already mastered framework joints, the mortise and tendon, and the mitre joint, West is keen to learn one of the strongest ways to connect timber. In the workshop Conrad shows West how to work a dovetail.

Conrad cuts the slopes with a tenon saw, holding the work in the bench vice. He moves the saw slowly, squarely, just touching the depth mark with the teeth. He then places the socket member into the vice with the dovetail part laid over it with a length of offcut supporting the far end.

📖 What if the joint is too loose? West asks.

– Can't do a lot. Adhesive is no use as contracts when dries. The best thing is put down to experience and start again.

Conrad is brave with the words, with the grinning facade. But West watches him speak and work with a different perspective now, having heard Conrad's tale the previous night, over cheddar and caffeine, under a humming Tilly lamp. West tries to imagine the small man living through the experiences he described. Experiences that seem too much to belong to the tanned face and upright frame standing by the bench.

Born in Arkhangel'sk, on the banks of the White Sea in Soviet Russia. Flat miles of industrial decay and archaic shipyards swept by the constant gales of rotting fish. Grey, square edifices planted in uneven rows upon the cold earth, built to withstand the extremes of an Arctic climate. Born into a family struggling to exist. A runt of a child, sickly, abandoned at the age of seven to an orphanage. They had no patience for the weak, dyslexic boy who would not be able to bring home a wage from the quay. In his first month at the home he was led into a blue room and forced to undress by a long man with glasses and beard, pushed over the table and raped.

Taken up by a quayside pimp, selling to itinerant sailors docking and loading then looking for sex on the desolate shores of the Dvina estuary. Seven years of filth, of degradation beyond the dogs who slept at his feet under tarpaulin. Then sold to various ships, kept in secret compartments onboard ship and shared between the crew. Eventually, he sighted land when he was upon the deck he was rarely allowed to visit, he saw his chance and leapt into the North Sea. Now, ten years later, the human flotsam laughs, smiles, works hard in the carpentry shop.

West listens to the breathing coming from Conrad's section of the caravan; the fight for inhalation, the heavy release. West is working late into the night on his signing. Plunged into learning the language with the same energy he gave to models, desperate to improve. He becomes more obsessive, watching his hands in reflection, exercising his fingers to develop suppleness, poring over pages of textbooks and manuals, living life through his gestures and nurtured signs. Night is the best time to study, the hazy candle adding a sense of adventure and secrecy to his education.

West stops for one moment to consider the future need for sign if the surgery frees his voice. Perhaps he'll be able to talk: banter, chat, natter, gossip, gab, converse, ask, command, whisper, query, joke, shout, sing. What about sing? West thinks. Strange to recall song. The last tunes were hollered out at seven when standing alongside his primary-school comrades. 'Bananas in Pyjamas'. 'Wide, Wide as the Ocean'. 'Lily the Pink'. Those high notes, the last chance to break his lungs open. The internal screams and throat roars that followed did not emancipate the emotions in the same way.

With a thin face and freed airways perhaps he'll be able to sleep on his side or on his front rather than forced to stare at ceilings. Perhaps able to hold each cheek and feel the push and pull of breath through his fingers. Perhaps he'll be able to open his mouth wide and take gulps of air, to savour it.

Secure at the Ranch, once finally settled, he will be able to contact East. Maybe, once his face is sliced back to some kind of normality, to features that East will not recognise. Features excavated from the layers of disease built over them. West envisages the conversation between them.

– Hello East, it's me.

– Who's me?

– West.

– What?

– Yes, brother, it's me. I've been under the knife.

– Oh my God, let me look at you, East would say, moulding the thin face in his grip. – What's happened? You look great.

– What, didn't I look good before? West smiles.

– Well not now that I've seen you like this.

– I think I look like you.

– Steady on, Westy, don't get carried away. You ain't that good looking.

– Dad?

– Yeah, I can see Dad.

What would East think of the beach? considers West. What would East think of the camp? Not enough action, not enough girls. Not enough city. East would see the space and flee.

For West, Stepney was just a camp pitched on the banks of the Mile End Road, shaping wood in the quiet of the flat, watching the debris accumulate on the flagstones below.

On the beach the next morning, under a foggy sun, the camp walks in an extended line. Hands dip into the sand to examine objects, holding shells to the sky, wiping crusty sheen off driftwood. Keith walks along the beach with his chest pushed out, arms swinging, not bothering to study the crunch underneath foot but keeping his stare fixed fifty metres ahead. He's looking for the big find, daring to overlook the miniature for the huge, lurching over the sand barefooted, still a soldier, wading into combat.

Conrad lags behind the line, continually falling to his knees to grapple with the beach, to wrench pipes, rope, timber out of the damp sand. Dragging his fingers through the seaweed and pebbles. Eager to fill his sack, to heap the most wood on to the scattered piles.

In the afternoon he teaches West the fundamentals of bending timber.

– All timber can be bent before it snaps. The amount of bend depends on type and thickness of the wood.

Conrad takes West to the timber store and finds two examples of bent wood.

– There are two ways of bending timber; one is soften by steaming and then bend. The other method is lamination.

They go to the work bench and prepare thin strips of timber, cutting across the grain of the outer veneers. The edges of the strips are glass-papered and then butted together to obtain the required length. Conrad strokes adhesive over the wood and places the compact lump into a baseboard to begin the bending process.

They stare at the wood, breathing in the pungent fumes of glue, waiting for it to fix. West turns to Conrad with his pad.

📖 Do you ever think of Russia?

– Every time I hear the horn from ship.

📖 Will you want to go back some day?

– I would like see Mother and Father again. But guess they are long time dead. Life is hard in Russia.

📖 You forgive them?

– Of course, they did not know better. They were peasants, city peasants. I sorry for not being who they wanted me to be.

📖 But they should have loved you regardless.

– How could they? They cannot choose emotions they have. Russia is hard.

West works in the afternoon alongside Meredith, building a bookcase from veneered chipboard. West collects the tools required: a light hammer, a fine-tooth panel saw, a try-square, a marking gauge, a marking knife, a $\frac{3}{4}$ inch bevel-edge chisel, a fine nail punch, a plough plane and a $\frac{1}{2}$ inch paring chisel.

Meredith, with blond hair pressed into a bunch on the top of her head, with long nose and pinched mouth. Just a few years older than West, she acknowledges him without an inquisitive stare. She throws smiles over clamped panels, and recurrent glances from coquettish eyes that West tries to ignore, unsure of the flattery, concentrating on the joint marking, the smooth and steady stroke of the chisel, the overlapping thrusts of the plough plane.

Meredith, with her infinite joy. Unnatural, thinks West. Something about her. Always a smile, a greeting, social cant. But there is something about her that West senses when the smile is turned off and her dreamy gaze becomes intense. Scratching and cursing the wood under the noise of the workshop only to resurface with the smile. At each side of the mouth West can see the strain, experienced eyes identify the stifled storm beneath.

West throws her a nod accompanied by a carefully executed point of the hand that asks, 'Are you okay?'

– I'm fine. Fine. Just can't seem to keep the wood in the vice, she replies, the smile weaker than ever.

West shows the thumb, returns to the plane.

– Can you show me? she asks.

He goes over and edges Meredith to one side. He adjusts the wood and shows her the best way to lock a vice with an awkwardly shaped piece of timber. She moves into him and allows her body to push against West's. He can feel her breath tickling his neck and ears.

Finished with the demonstration, he pats her on the hand and returns to his bench. Meredith does not return to her work but keeps focused on West, his erect biceps pushing tools along the wood, his blue iris flashing from her to the wood, to her, back to the wood. She wipes her mouth with a sawdusty hand, her mind freed from the clamped timber on to West who is made nervous by the attention but, because of it, realises that he is already yearning for another.

8

Geezer and Bloke are sitting in the living room of the family house on Jubilee Street. Sucking on bottled beer and stretched over sofa and armchair. The house is quiet without Mother and Sister (shopping), Father (at the business), Snickers (the pet terrier sleeping in the backyard kennel).

Life has not been the same since the death. Mother keeps crying, Father keeps shouting, Sister keeps trying too hard to pretend that nothing has happened.

Geezer places his bottle on to the coffee table.

– Boy, how do they make that taste so good?

Bloke smiles and smells the top of his drink to enhance the beer swilling about his mouth.

It is the first time in a month the brothers have been alone together at home. There is a desire to talk about Girl, to talk about East, but neither brother is willing to instigate the conversation about the shared concern. Each day they wait for the phone call to announce East's death, but no one in the house admits to the adrenalin surge when ringing breaks the endless waiting.

Geezer returns to the bottle, sliding it into hand and on to lips in a single sweeping move. Bloke sips in tandem, takes a long swallow and tries to appear comfortable.

– Going to the Horse tonight? Bloke asks.

– I'll nip down for one or two.

– What you up to tomorrow? Bloke asks.

– See what Dad wants ... if he wants anything. I can't get through to him.

– I thought he wanted you to head over Canning Town and settle up with Cash and Carry Harry.

– Who the fuck knows? I couldn't make out a word the last time we spoke. I'm just keeping my head down. I'm scared

what I'm going to do to him if he keeps on screaming at me.
I'm filling up, I can't keep smiling.

– He hasn't been shouting at me, Bloke says, lowering the
bottle and resting it on the arm of the chair.

– That's because you haven't been here, haven't been
helping, as usual.

– Omit it, Geeze. Don't blame me for the fuck-ups you're
making.

– Fuck-ups? Geezer sneers, sitting up on the sofa. – Tell me
more about my fuck-ups.

– Well, why d'you think the old man is shouting at you?
Why d'you think the old dear can't stop crying?

– Because of me, you say?

– You know you aren't finishing things, let's just leave it at
that.

– You cocky cunt, are you withholding?

– Let's not go there.

Geezer moves into a seated position, his elbows resting on
knees.

– We're already there, explain yourself before I rip you up,
he says.

– Well, where's East, where's our buddy East, eh?

– You know what's going on there.

– You chose the fucking cripple, not me, Bloke replies,
looking away from Geezer. – I would have got someone who
could do the job.

– Am I believing this? You're telling me that the reason
Mum, Dad and the rest of you are on my case is because I got
Withered Arm on the job and he hasn't finished it yet. Is that
right?

– The guy can't even hold a fucking rifle.

– He's an old comrade, Dad was happy with him.

– The guy can't even use a fucking garrotte. The only hit

man in history who can only wear slip-on shoes and Velcroed clothes!

– You weren't complaining when he took out Ronny Market. In fact, come to think of it, you were the first bod in the queue waiting to buy him a bevvy down the pub.

– It hardly took a criminal genius to get a man pissed and then stamp on his head twenty-eight, thirty or however many times. Nice work, yeah, nice job well done. Give the man a fucking banana but don't give me the big one about talent.

– Dave-Boy Dennis?

– Roll again, he left one of the bastard's hands lying in the middle of the road!

Geezer shakes his head and stands up, stretching himself up into the lampshade. The bottle of beer is left half drunk on the table.

– I'm not going to tear you up because you're fucked off like the rest of us. But I'm telling you, just once, get off me, yeah? Get off me, little brother, because when that body comes back and all scores are settled I know you are going to be back in the front of that queue buying me and Withered a drink.

Jacob's Lad

1

West has joined more of Mary's BSL classes. Now he attends on Monday, Wednesday and Thursday nights. Evenings are spent discussing sport, the arts, politics, hobbies, through the silent language. West continues to learn new words, new interpretations, captured in gesture or spelt out in letters: superfluous, irritating, tragic, precious, subtle, persuasive, fading, penetrating, captured, orchard, tidal, coastal, acid, terse.

West can stay late after class now that Keith stays at the Ranch and allows West to take a taxi. Mary and West share each other over lukewarm drinks, always last to leave before the caretaker sweeps under their feet and brushes them towards cloakroom, foyer, finally the door.

Monday night. Mary stands by the classroom door politely seeing off the students, waiting for West to arrive last and for them to walk to the drinks machine, leaving the empty classroom behind. Childhood, school, the East End, family, work, hopes, music, models – Mary prises West open with her concern. And in turn, West returns the curiosity with an interrogation of his own – her childhood, school, home town and family. Both try to outdo each other with the questions, asking before being asked, asking instead of answering, keen to take control of the conversation, to show more interest. To make the other feel more important.

West cannot believe that he has told her about the Berserkers, about the time capsule, his dad's punch, the Face Facts picture. She cannot believe that she has told him about her father's adultery, about her sterility, about her divorce ten years previously. Mary responded reluctantly, as if West would not care. – Oh, he left me years ago. As if he would not be interested. – He was too selfish. As if he would not sympathise. – We couldn't have children. He wanted them so badly that my failure became his rejection.

Both Mary and West are throwing out their souls to be caught in the nets of each other's concern. They often become so intense that Mary stops signing and speaks, leaving West to communicate in silence alone.

The silence is dense on this evening when Mary takes the conversation from concern and compassion into compliment.

– You're an amazing person, West. A beautiful person.

And the communication stops, the quick-fire questions, the reactive replies become echoes emptied into the deserted building. Mary and West fill the silence with a stare, clutching drained coffee cups, and unwilling to acknowledge that it is time to go. Mary reddens, the sixty-year-old skin fights the shame of the stare. West feels his knees tremble, his hands tighten on the cup to dampen the shakes. An audible swallow, digesting the moment.

Wednesday night. Mary waits by the door and West waits at his desk. They listen to the flurry of footfalls down the hollow corridor, clicking and dragging to the stairwell. Mary appears more apprehensive than usual, watching the final swings of the pushed doorway. The hair is tightly pulled behind, no loose hairs slip out, the lipstick is brighter, the skin more evenly covered in foundation. Her blouse is slightly looser about the chest, revealing a golden chain with pendant, revealing dark brown flesh, darker than her face and hands.

West approaches Mary at the door, unable to muster the casual greeting of the previous Monday, of the previous weeks. Unable to break out of the awkward silence imposed on him by fear. He tries a few simple signs but his hands do not move with fluency or fluidity.

Mary seems to accept the awkwardness, the nervousness, and replies with a clearing of the throat. She is hardly able to look at the lumpy face in front of her. Not out of disgust, but out of her own diffidence. Both Mary and West have spent the past two nights and two days thinking of each other's faces, trying to construct every line, feature, expression, so able to admire and desire in private the person they have come to know.

🖐 Coffee? Mary manages, casting her gaze to the grey linoleum flooring.

🖐 Or perhaps a drink elsewhere? West signs.

West forces himself to look Mary in the eye, refuses to submit to the timidity that urges him to turn away, to run away.

🖐 That would be lovely, Mary replies.

The relief spills over her face, washing over West and taking with it the mutual fear now transformed into energy.

Hunstanton is wet under drizzle, glistening beneath the bruised sky. They walk from the college to the town centre, avoiding puddles, dripping trees and cars driving too close to the flooded kerbs. Nothing is said or communicated as they stamp down the hill, forcing their feet to act as brakes as the gradient increases.

The Black Horse, emanating a yellow glow and the hum of

midweek drinking, stands on the corner of the main road, overlooking the Green, the promenade and the sea. Mary and West acknowledge the name with a point and a nod. Not such an uncommon name, but they both still smile.

Heads turn to West as he waits at the bar, fiddling with a ten pound note. Mary stands behind, head down, lacking her teacher's confidence now she's out of the classroom. West does not notice her shyness, he's waiting for the landlord to catch the waving tenner.

Sitting, sipping, signing, scribbling through the ripples of other people's conversations. Pint of Beck's, with straw. Vodka and tonic, with ice. Both glasses pushed about the table, a ouija board marked by wet stains. Barely an inch between the thighs, bodies squeezed on to a bench between beams. Barely a foot between the two faces, one slight and open, the other bulbous, closed by skin. But Mary is not interested in studying the layers of curved flesh, she maintains her focus on the bright blue marble squinting out from beneath a falling forehead, a crumbling cliff-face. She watches West relax and form shapes, form patterns with his hands, form patterns with his life that he has never done before. He is able to explore the past, almost as if looking down on the life of another. Detached and perceptive as he describes a deformed life through gestures and notepad without the emotional nuances of speech. At the Ranch he is banned from discussing the past, they prefer people to look to the sun, despite Keith's and Conrad's tales that seem to recur week after week.

Generally, throughout the camp, there is a conspiracy of silence. Backs are turned to shadows. Keith urges West to forget all that is behind him. Discussed, dissected, discarded, for it is the Ranch that offers a future. Hope founded in

Holme, in coastal wind, in communal cabin, in carpentry shop.

Mary is happy to nurse the vodka – her car is still parked at the college – and share a compelling friendship with West. He examines her skin, the discreet thread veins on nose and cheek. The way she strokes her fingers before replying as she waits to lead West, with a sign, into a new region of self-assessment. Before West startles at his self-absorption and turns the inquisition on to Mary. And then she slides her drink into a new puddle, smearing the spillage before returning her glass to its original position.

Back at the camp, West listens to Conrad sleep and thinks of Mary. Now he's incapable of escaping from his desire. Forty years of difference, yet with so much to give, so much warmth. The touch of her hands as she guides him into new finger formations. He tries to push away his emotions, represses the fantasy of his ugliness pressed against her patterned dress. Yet, sleepless in the night, his mind retraces its steps back to the craving. Back to the thrill of being with Mary who allows him to be himself, to see himself, who encourages him to shape the past into something solid.

2

On the beach the following morning they find a dog. Without legs. Chewing on its own lips as it gasps for air and water. At first Meredith thinks it is a pile of clothes, before it coughs water. Before its eyes, rimmed with deposited salt, blink and stream liquid.

The animal does not appear to be in pain, the sea water has numbed its amputations. Yet it is clearly in distress, drifted in with the tide from an unknown place. From across the Wash? From a ship? Meredith clutches the heap of wet pelage and runs over the sand towards the camp.

Conrad and West fetch water and a plate of cold meat from the kitchen. The three of them wipe off splashes as the dog laps furiously at the bowl. Meredith holds the animal while West and Conrad rub the sodden coat with a towel. The dog vomits back into the bowl and suddenly loses the strength to continue.

– She's dying, she's dying, Meredith says to West, gently shaking the dog to encourage the intake of more liquid.

Keith arrives and takes the dog from Meredith's grasp. He lifts it up and examines the head and body, like an adult looking for the off-switch on a child's toy.

– We'll have to kill it.

– You can't kill her, Meredith protests.

– It alive, Conrad says.

– Look at it, Keith replies. – There's no hope for it, it'd be cruel to let it live.

– No, you can't just kill her, Meredith insists, hidden anger pushing through the seams of her argument.

The dog, oblivious to the significance of the debate, sighs and begins to open and shut its jaw. Stretching the mouth in an attempt to inhale more oxygen. Dying in Keith's arms before he can take it to the workshop and drive a drill into its skull.

– See, it's dead, Keith says, handing the dog back to Meredith who places it gently on the floor.

Keith can see Meredith's volcanic glare as she struggles to maintain composure.

– Easy, Meredith. I didn't kill it.

– But you wanted it to die!

– I did not, I thought it would be best, Keith argues back,

straightening himself to his full height – an instinctive reaction to assault.

– You make me ...

Then Keith reaches out and holds Meredith by the shoulders.

– Easy.

Meredith's face breaks apart. She wipes at her hair collected in a bunch on the top of her head. She brushes it upwards to wipe away her distress and Keith's restraining arms.

Keith walks off, back to the beach. Conrad, Meredith and West stand about the animal and stare at the drowned pile. All of them notice that the dog does not have a tail. Severed, like the legs, and replaced by a festering wound, closed red and sore by the hours spent bobbing on waves.

Meredith takes the opportunity to reach for West. She drapes her arms over his shoulders and pulls her head onto his neck. West stands awkwardly, stunned by the intimacy of the girl who brushes past his bench with slight touches, and stares at him as he works and eats. The dead dog and the anger at Keith excuse the lunge, and the two of them remain fixed while Conrad watches.

In the afternoon, Conrad and West build a coffin for the dog, despite Keith's insistence that no coffin is necessary. – It's only a bloody dog. Meredith does not look at Keith, she bites her fingernails as she stares at the grass.

They use pine, with dovetail and skew nailing, lifting the hammer bruises from the wood with a heated iron and damp cloth. Gluing the paring back into position after the nail is fixed. Fitting the lid with battens slotted inside the two end panels. West feels content at the bench, with wood and a purpose, building a box for the dead dog. Brushed by Meredith, the fur groomed smooth over its back and sides, the dog is put into the lacquered crate looking clean, despite the jaw locked in a desperate lunge.

3

Meredith, the coffin, the evening class, another evening at the Black Horse in Hunstanton behind him, West enters Mary's house. Four pints cannot calm the thumping panic as he pushes the door into the latch. Watching Mary's figure, smooth and soft under cotton, lead him through a hallway of mirrors and wooden side-tables into a lounge decorated in warm pastels and flower paintings.

– So this is where I call home, she says, with her back to West.

A shortness of breath and the rush to swallow betray her nervousness. She undrapes the cardigan from around her shoulders and dismisses it on to a dining chair at one end of the room. Mary appears flushed, from the vodkas, from the sound of West's heavy breathing.

West lowers himself clumsily on to the settee, desperate to break the stifling silence with an interesting sign or note, though his mind is blank.

Mary pours two tumblers of whisky, glass tapping against glass. West follows the line of her leg under the light dress, to an exposed ankle bent into a black shoe. He feels at her mercy, as in their conversations, she dictates the way in which West explores his experiences.

His yearning to touch her undermines his casual demeanour and imposes upon him a stiffness that Mary has noticed even with her back turned. She ignores two armchairs and chooses to sit alongside him on the settee. He grasps the glass, holding the straw with a finger, and scours the room for a subject, afraid to look Mary in the eye, and forgetting even the most basic signs when he decides to compliment the picture adorning the wall.

Mary, too, avoids West's gaze. Aware of his reluctance, his distance, as she tips the glass on to her lips and rebukes herself for having invited such a scene. Embarrassing West, humiliating herself as some kind of perverted pensioner with unnatural, unfair designs on such a young man afflicted by disease. She pushes herself against the arm of the sofa, creating the maximum distance between herself and her guest for whom she cares too much. A concern illustrated by the pile of books in her bedroom on neurofibromatosis, dumbness, London. Books she has studied so that she can offer empathy. In secret, though.

West notices the trouble on Mary's face. Perhaps he should not have agreed to a nightcap, perhaps he was unable to recognise a polite invitation, not meant to be accepted. He sucks hard on the straw and flinches at the kick from the spirit that forces tears into his eyes, aggravated by his tight throat.

☙ I'd better be off.

☙ Shall I call you a taxi? she signs.

☙ No, I'll walk.

The front door closes behind West and his anger opens as he steps into the darkness. So angry with himself for being so silent, so detached. He was in her home, next to her on the sofa. At night. Eleven o'clock. Close enough to smell the rosy hints of her, to see the flesh of her ankle. Frustrated by his desire, how it confined him and made him sit without a clue as to commonplace discussion or friendship. The days and nights of fantasy, of him and Mary alone just as they had been.

The lights of the house still beam as he walks into the

darkness, watching his muddled shape on the pavement. Back into the shadows, not where he wants to be, not where he should be now that the Ranch has shown him how to face the light.

He stops walking and waits for his thoughts to clear. Why should he accept his failure? Here in Norfolk he has found a sense of himself, a sense of being. He's no longer resigned to the sidelines of other lives. Now is the time to break out of the safety of failure and take responsibility for his own circumstances. Tonight, in the pub with Mary, he grasped the elements of his desire; the intimacy, the belonging, the happiness. And he acknowledged his physical craving that accompanied every sign and expression, down to the examination of her eyelids as she blinked between thoughts.

He turns towards the house and jogs back to the door. The eerie chime of the bell. The painful wait for a figure to emerge behind coloured glass panels. The taste of whisky still on his tongue. The shared expressions of relief as she peeks from behind the chain and fiddles with the catch to open the door.

👐 I just wanted to say that I am sorry for being so quiet earlier. I don't know what was the matter with me.

West stands in the hallway, Mary pushes the door shut and turns to him.

– Oh, West, I thought it was me. I thought it was me.

👐 No, no. I did not want to go, I just felt that I was doing things wrong.

– Perhaps we both felt like that.

👐 This is difficult.

Mary watches West's face look to the floor, she feels his dejection. But she, too, feels the need to touch.

– Do you want to stay? she offers quietly, almost as an apology.

þ You must be tired.

Mary smiles, shakes her head so slightly in recognition of West's forced but genuine concern.

– Don't you want to stay with me?

West pauses, ambushed by Mary's directness and his own want that makes him hesitate and allows the guilt to speak for him.

– I want you to stay, Mary says, intimately, urging West to crack under the interrogation, under the light. Urging him to admit his feelings.

West can feel his legs shudder and he can hardly bear to tear his gaze off the carpet. It's gently prised away by Mary's hand stroking his jaw and pushing his face up to look at her. West is shaking all over, his hands can barely hold her.

Mary's dress falls to the carpet with a cotton whisper.

4

Meredith sits with West in her caravan, decorated with bright red curtains and orange cushions. They've broken off from the carpentry after a difficult morning trying to fit the legs on to a chair.

She takes West's hands and strokes them.

– Such lovely hands. Not as beaten up as mine. There again, I have been working in the shop for a few years.

Her voice is like her smile; some kind of disguise that West cannot uncover. She speaks clearly, her voice is almost plummy, yet there is the hint of West Country or Birmingham in the vowels. West is aware of the way that she cannot keep eye contact for more than a few seconds at a time, her gaze darts off to the side, or above, or below, for gasps of visual air. Occasionally her eyelids will blink rapidly, the eyeballs roll up into the skull and reappear fully dilated in astonished mode.

West prises his hands free and takes the notepad.

📖 How did you become so good with wood?

– I just took to it, like you did. It was either wood or working in the allotments or the kitchen. I had to take to it, if you look at it in that way.

She offers a rapid flicker of eyelids and a slight snigger, which West accepts with knowing nods. He does not understand the extent to which his personality has superseded the deformity while at the Ranch. To others, without West's past, her attentiveness would be pleasing, exciting even. But West does not connect with attractive girls touching him and embracing him and inviting him for coffee. On occasions there is the scent of sympathy, of mothering, yet Meredith's attention is intense and passionate.

But it is Mary for whom West craves, and with Meredith sitting next to him, smothering him with longing, it is a matter of honour and honesty to slip further along the seat and away from her fawning touch.

– She's too old for you, Meredith suddenly says.

Meredith knows the truth; the Ranch spreads gossip. The atmosphere in the caravan changes, the subtlety of her touch and movements are replaced by agitation and repressed rage.

West can think of nothing to add, unsure as to whether the accusation is to be construed as offensive or as an offer of Meredith's own availability. Confounded by his sudden involvement in female passion he bows his head as if in prayer, not wanting to harm friendship.

– In fact, it's disgusting! she hisses; once again the smiling facade is shoved aside by emotion.

She's a time bomb, thinks West. That's what it is. The easy smiles are comforting ticks.

Meredith could not prevent the silence igniting the pain, now she attacks West with more insults. She is determined to incite a response, a regret, a hand that will reach out for her. But West will not yield, will not proffer a grip that will pull him and Mary into abyss. And so he stands to go, leaves a note.

📖 I'm sorry.

Sorry for Meredith, sorry for Mary ('It's disgusting!'), sorry for himself having to spend his life apologising for his emotions, his desires, his decisions.

– So what's it like touching an old lady?

Now the envy burns, flaming at West who is stunned by the violence of her words. He turns abruptly from his departure, stabs her with a stare, held for an extra second for emphasis.

– Or touching saggy tits?

He shuts the door with a calm push.

– What is it with her? Look at me for once, look at me!

Killing Time

1

East rips open the letter from Leafy to reveal a page torn from a newspaper. An advertisement. DUMB, UGLY (AND HOMELESS). East stares at the horror, disbelieving. He takes the accompanying letter and glances over the spidery ink. Leafy has waited three months for West to write, to relieve her concerns after reading the advert. West had assured her that he had a job, a home, but the lies were exposed by the desperate portrait. She had waited three months in the belief that a letter would come, but now she has lost patience. All her letters to the P.O. box have gone unanswered. Now she fears for the poor boy, homeless in Cambridge.

Three months! East is furious at Leafy's secrecy when she knew how much he yearned for his brother. But there's no time now for vicious words. Time to head for Cambridge and find West. Perhaps the Garners have found him already? East vows murder if West is hurt.

East carries his bag to King's Cross station and struggles to find trains out of the capital to Cambridge. East leaves behind the security of the metropolis in which he operates most effectively: roaming the urban acres, the Roman roads slicing up the spread of city.

East is determined to collect his brother and plan a suitable survival. He plans a straightforward meeting at Face Facts, a reunion with West and then a train back out. He imagines West homeless on the streets, stuck on benches with the rotting figures East knows from outside the Salvation Army on Whitechapel Road or has seen shuffling along Charing Cross Road on his way to Soho on a weekend mission with the Stepney boys. How he wishes to relive those days, be part of the past, clinking jars with Tops, brushing the thighs of a Spanish au pair in a Bond Street boozer, lying on the sofa at home with buttered toast and mugged tea watching a film with big Clint – a Wild West warrior in the same mould as his Tower Hamlets confederates. To bowl along to Bow. To march to Mile End. To wander about Wapping. To pop into Poplar. To lurch around Limehouse. To see the Canary Wharf tower standing straight and tall, blinking like a lighthouse, warning outsiders away from the rocky coast of the East End. Where East so wants to be.

Neil at Face Facts offers little in the way of assistance. He is suspiciously unhelpful as he suggests East visit the tribes of homeless that live about the town. That knew West. That may have seen him before he left.

East is pointed from corner to alley, face to face, to a legless man called Toby, who responds reluctantly to East's questions.

– I've already had his brother here ages ago, says Toby.

– What the fuck?

– Big bloke, funny arm.

East knew the three months was too long to wait.

East remembers his bag; the passport, the driving licence, which he shows to Toby who bites his lip and realises his mistake.

Despite the risk of revenge from the closing clan, he has to get to his brother; months apart have left too many holes. He wants to hear the tap of pen on pad, see the squint, feel the enveloping aura. East is desperate to ensure that he is safe.

2

Withered Arm is in Hunstanton, following Toby's directions, living in a bed and breakfast, waiting for West to join his brother, lure his brother, betray his brother. Whatever way, Withered Arm is there to fire the gun or stick the blade when East is revealed.

He has watched West through binoculars, walking on the beach and disappearing inside the safety of the Ranch's borders. He has followed West to the doctor, dentist, college and pub. He has seen West and Mary naked through the window at night. He was there the evening the affair began, when West went to the house, left the house, and returned to the house.

He has been phoning Geezer, sleeping when he has the chance, living off chips and chocolate, propositioning the landlady, watching weeks turn to months with no sign of renegade brother. He is tiring of the wait while impatient Geezer threatens. Grabbing a drink in seafront pubs, describing himself as a consultant, as a man from Brighton, though he finds it hard to resist a Kray story when bar-stool conversation turns to crime.

– Let me tell you about Ginger Marks ...

Later in the quiet of the boarding house, he turns his mind to inner thoughts. To affirmation.

> I will kill East
> The Garners will thank me
> I will be the best killer in the world
> I will capture East
> I will kill East

3

East watches the tracts of cultivated land glide past the window of the train to Hunstanton. The sun bleaches the land and East thinks of Jerome in Victoria Park. Last summer, when a crowd of them took two cars up there for the day. Absorbing the sun and smoking cigarettes, taking the piss out of each other. Bloke and East eyed Jerome suspiciously as he walked over to two girls lying on towels near by and began a conversation. Jerome was not a stud, and the rest of the crew sat and watched with intrigue as he slouched and joked in front of the females. He turned to look at his mates with a cocky sneer. That marked his card. Within seconds the friends were on top of him, unbuttoning his trousers and ripping off his shirt. They stripped him naked and threw his clothes into a tree. The girls and the crew laughed as Jerome ran behind a bin and begged for help.

– Don't you try and come it with us, Bloke said, with a cigarette hanging from his lip.

East sits on the train and lets out a nasal chuckle. It still seems funny, despite the new circumstances. It also seems distant, from a different age.

The giraffe woman is reluctant to open the gate of the Ranch. The camp is for those seeking refuge not those seeking relatives.

– But he's my brother, East reiterates, retorts, until the woman relents. He is taken to Keith in the cabin.

Keith looks at East across the table, studies the passport, the licence.

– Why have you come to find him?

– Because he's my brother, we got split up, there was a bit of a mix-up.

– Why didn't West contact you? Keith asks.

– You'll have to ask him.

Keith agrees to a brief meeting between the brothers, it is rare for relations to come knocking. Such gate-calls are usually prevented by uncertainty, fear or the secrecy of the Ranch. Like East, there are some who find their way to Holme with peaceful intentions, and there are others with more violent ones. Some incursions, intent on kidnap or retake, are repelled by Keith's Smith & Wesson or, as happened once before, by Ranch residents taking up kitchen knives, hoes, rakes, forks and the tools hanging in the carpentry shop in which West now stands working.

The large head is bent over a trestle, the softwood steadied by a knee, a forefinger points alongside the blade of a panel saw as it slices through timber in steady strokes.

East hesitates at the door, struck rigid by the sight of his brother, the lumpy back of his head bowed in concentration. He does not go over to West but waits at the entrance, waits for Keith to tap his brother on the arm.

Lowering the saw, flinching out of working trance, following the point of a finger, West turns to East.

– How are you doing, bro? East says, now stepping into the artificial light of the carpentry shed.

West puts the tool down on the bench, looks at Keith, looks back to East. The swollen head tints scarlet, a nervous sweep of the hair and West glances, without thinking, a look that East still recognises as 'Fuck me!'. East's face opens into pleasure as he moves towards West and wraps his brother in embrace.

The remainder of the afternoon is spent catching up, and then patching up the past months apart. East is so relieved that West is untouched by the hunter who's living near by and waiting for East to arrive.

Now both of the brothers sit in the caravan sharing tea served from a pot. Both East and West perspire on the foam seats, from the hot tea, from the heat of surprise that they should be here together. Both safe, both flushed.

Conrad pops his head into the heat and waves to the brothers before closing the door and leaving them to talk.

East tells West about the impostor in Cambridge, who now knows about the Ranch and is undoubtedly waiting for the chance to take him out of the game.

– You'd better pack your stuff, Westy. The sooner we get out of here the better.

West tilts his head to question East's presumption. The answer put on paper, like before, no attempt at signing for East.

📖 I'm not going anywhere.

– What are you talking about? We gotta get out of here. Someone has followed you here.

📖 Yes, you have. I'm staying.

East slams the cup down, anger spilling over on to the table with the tea.

– I don't fucking believe you, West. I've come all this way to sort you out, make sure you're safe, and you don't give a fuck!

West maintains his composure, the blue iris stays fixed on his brother, unblinking. Then he turns to pen and paper.

📖 This is my home now. I'm settled, I'm doing good.

– It's full of a bunch of wankers, fucking losers, if you ask me.

📖 I didn't ask you. Just like you've never asked me.

– Someone is out there trying to kill us!

West gives time for his brother to simmer, to release his grip on the cup.

📖 I'll take my chances. I've been here long enough. If they wanted me they could have taken me.

– Westy, I need you to come with me.

📖 I've met someone.

– What? A girl?

📖 A woman.

– Oh, for fuck's sake.

West explains, noticing East swallow his fury with the dregs of the tea, followed by a shudder.

East is overcome with envy at his brother's love for a woman, though he remains silent, restrained from criticism by the enthusiasm exploding from West's gestures, pen pressed into pad and indenting the blank pages below with his feeling. East is aware that he has never seen his brother so alive, so ecstatic, inside a caravan with its anachronistic decor and the smell of plastic.

West is happy to see East. Perhaps the premature arrival has taken away a little of the pleasure from inviting East himself. Yet he always looked forward to the reunion.

Being next to the sneering smile and impatient slang returns West to the past and back to so much of what the Ranch is trying to put behind. But East was his brother, not a shadow, although he did look different sitting in the caravan in clothes West had not seen before, with hair grown out of the crop into a thick mat. The good-looking face is thinner and more bony, with dark rings around the eyes.

West could detect East's reaction to Mary, and he did not mind. He understood the fear of the older brother watching the younger grow self-reliant. He has shown East the man he has become. And then he tells East of the man he could become if he wanted to have the surgery outlined by the consultant. The chance to have a smooth face and, perhaps, clear voice. The chance to unmask and become normal.

– This is getting ridiculous. A camp of freaks, an old biddy as a bird, and now some fucking leech is going to rip your face to shit.

📖 I know all this is weird.

– You don't want to change who you are! East protests. – You don't want to change what God has made you.

West urges East to stay at the camp, within the security of the runaway community. That way he will be able to mingle with the Ranchers, meet Mary, visit the consultant with him and express his concerns.

East sits back at the table in the cabin, facing Keith, explaining the situation, explaining the truth of Girl Garner, of the man who has certainly followed West to Holme.

– They'll be watching out for me, I can tell you that.

– Then we'll just have to keep a better watch out on you.

– They'll have been waiting for me to arrive, treating West like bait. I bet they spy through the fence, keep an eye on the beach. I know these people, they're not a bunch of mugs.

– You'll just have to keep your head down. You'll be all right.

Keith accepts East for two weeks on condition that he, in return, accepts work in the kitchen as part of the community.

– I don't do that kind of work, that's not my scene at all, East argues.

Keith outlines the unsuitability of the other work: unable to walk on the beach for fear of the hit man, no carpentry skills, the vegetable and fruit gardens too near the perimeter hedge.

– The kitchen is the only spot. You could always be in charge of the toilets?

Two weeks at the camp will allow East to spend time with his brother and make surreptitious visits with West to the surgeon. A chance, so Keith foresees, to be seduced by the safety and freedom available to those tired of running. Keith is enthused by the prospect of a healthy guy, a guy like himself in many ways, moving in and becoming one of them.

– You've certainly got enough problems to be admitted, Keith says, laughing.

– Cheers, replies East.

– Serious, we could use someone like you around here.

– No fucking chance. I'm no loser.

– What, like your brother?

– You know what I mean.

– Nothing wrong with making a better life for yourself.

– Running away is not a better life. I've fucking tried it.

– You probably went to the wrong place.

– It's the principle of it not the places.

– Who says that?

– Common sense. Loser at home, loser away. Just in front of different people.

– Give us a chance. You'll see.

Even if Keith has his doubts about the putative executioner encamped on the dunes waiting months for the vague possibility of East's arrival, he dismisses them and takes out the Smith & Wesson from inside his jacket, placing it on the table in front of East.

– Just a precaution, have to be careful of anyone who comes through that gate. Just in case you thought it was all a bit lax.

– Nice shooter. Same one as the bloke who shot John Lennon.

– I can assure you it wasn't me.

The two of them laugh, shake hands, light cigarettes and discuss Keith's shadows.

– I was in the Falklands ...

East and West spend the night in the same half of the caravan talking about recent events rather than sleeping, whispering over the rustles and coughs of Conrad. Sharing words and notes and whispers and laughs and, later, moments of melancholy as they consider the unkempt graves. Finally they collapse into warm duvet, too warm for East who throws it aside with sweating gasps, to dream of changed lives, accompanied by the peacocks screeching outside.

Two weeks for East to taste the salt carried from the beach and into the noses and mouths of those at the camp. To experience the fulfilment West has found between the trees and waves at Holme. To meet Mary, maybe. To meet the surgeon, perhaps. To experiment with forgetting the past, moving into a different light, one that shines through thinner air and softer clouds than the dirty sky of home.

East spends the first two days sweating and wiping in the kitchen; assigned to domestic duties as agreed. Scrubbing at huge pans and peeling potatoes, lifting gas bottles in and out of ovens. Stepping on soaked grass amid the smell of wood. Talking to Enid, the giraffe woman, who refuses to discuss her shadows while East recounts the history of Stepney.

– I suppose we are all just reflections of our environment, suggests Enid.

– We were brought up hard, says East. – Brought up to take it on the chin.

– Isn't avoiding the blow better?

– I grew up with a few fighters and you're right about that. Hit and not get hit, that's the name of the game, East replies, fumbling about the sink for the last plate. He pulls out the dish and rinses it under cold water.

Enid stands hunched over the gas rings, her thin frame straining to lift a large pot over to the serving tables. West, Meredith and Conrad file in from the workshop for lunch, holding the metal trays full of potato salad made with home-grown spuds, home-made mayonnaise and home-cut chives. Trays full of slices of cold ham, and sliced tomatoes drizzled in oil. East heaves extra on to the mashed pile prepared for West who winks, pats his shoulder and swaggers to the table next to Conrad where they sit and share hand signals over plastic cupfuls of orange squash. They are joined by Meredith. West has accepted her apologies for the Mary saga and she is content to sit by Conrad and wait for inclusion in the hand gestures and occasional notes. She is willing to bide her time, not force the issue.

After lunch the brothers are allowed to spend time in the caravan, East continually looking into the hedges and towards the unmanned gate. He fails to concentrate on West's writing, but is content to be away from the kitchen and share his brother's air. The months of concern and panic for the missing West are forgotten now that the brother is beside him looking healthy and beaming blue from the single clear eye.

West, too, is happy being with his brother, particularly now that it is he who is in control, at home, among his people. He has noticed East's lack of attention, lack of response to his surroundings; he makes no mention of the vibrant greens of nature, the scent of sea and cloud, the crisp taste of the water. It is not just the effect of running, the effect of the recent events. It is not the kitchen. It is not just the expectation of a death squad waiting for him in Norfolk. It is deeper, more awful, emanating out of East like fire, making both of them sweat in the caravan despite the early autumn chill.

After supper, washing in the bathroom huts, a walk about the camp (keeping away from the hedge), watching the glitter appear on the night dome; East is still dripping and lies awake on his back while West watches the tears of sweat stream from his brother's head and on to the pillow.

4

Another day behind stoves and tables, clearing ketchup bottles from the breakfast tables, polishing knives and forks with a tea towel and placing them back into the plastic container ready for lunch. Fighting the fever swarming over his body and face, reducing his energy, continually using the kitchen cloths to absorb the perspiration. Removing his shirt and working bare-chested in front of Enid who excuses the hygiene implications and waits for a word with Keith.

West, meanwhile, is working on a set of dining chairs with Meredith. He is thinking of Mary. Drilling into a softwood, turning screws firmly into the joints, smoothing the wood flesh with glass-paper. Catching Meredith's eye, twitching under the overhanging hair, that affectionate gaze with which she assaults him. Watching the way she pulls the hammer back with a rapid series of mini blows before releasing the head back on to the nail. West is hoping East will fall in love with the camp. He's waiting to see him at meal time – see his confident grin as he shovels cabbage. Then, waiting to leave the Ranch for the evening class. To hold Mary's hand as they share a tumbler of whisky at her home before stepping up the stairs to the scents of sheet, blanket, bedspread. To lie on top of her.

Mary's hair is hanging loose over her face, she turns on her side and her breasts slide down. She strokes West's face, running her fingertips over some of the more severe mounds and through the hair pushed apart from other lumps.

– I'd like to meet your brother, she says.

West is exhausted, and he struggles to lift his hands to sign. Occasionally he forgets a word and is prompted by Mary, the word guessed at before he attempts clarification with a spelling.

👐 He is a star.

– I wonder what he'll think of you and me.

👐 Who cares?

– Do you think he would?

👐 He cares in a different way to other people.

West arrives back at the camp, acknowledges the others drinking hot chocolate in the cabin. He arrives at the caravan to find his brother drenched on the bed, in underpants, apologising for the cigarette smoke and flicking the butt out of the window.

📖 What's up?

– Nothing.

📖 I know something's up.

– I can't fucking take it, Westy. I just want to go home.

📖 Why don't you make this your home? It's got everything.

East doesn't say anything.

📖 We could find you a girl!

East smiles. East coughs. He sits up and stares at West.

– There's only ever one home.

📖 It takes time.

– Fuck off it does. I know where my home is, and it ain't here.

📖 But you haven't tried.

– I haven't tried cutting my arm off but I know I wouldn't like it. I'm not like all these freaks who've never had anything. They all think this place is great because they've never been happy. I was happy, West. I know what's out there and it's a fuck sight better than this shithole.

The door closes and West's silhouette walks towards the spotlights of the cabin.

– Westy, I'm sorry, I wasn't talking about you. I wasn't—

The shouted words collide with the shut door.

By two a.m. West is dreaming and East sits on the step of the caravan. His black hair is rubbed into a tangle, collecting in damp clumps. He waves a book in front of him to cool down despite the night chill. Walks barefooted to the shower huts and sinks under the cold water, almost detecting the hiss of extinguished heat. Propping his arms against the tiles and bending over to stare at his feet. Then clutching the nozzle like a microphone and thrusting his face into the jet.

He's back on the step at three a.m., oblivious to the piercing squeals of the peacocks, disturbed only by an approaching shape. At first East jolts with images of payback and gets ready to dive into the caravan, but the familiar figure of Keith soon emerges from the half-light. He's dressed in combat fatigues, his face smeared in camouflage stick; the blacks and greens of warfare.

– Can't sleep? Keith asks.

– I don't feel right.

East watches as Keith slips the Smith & Wesson into the tunic.

– I often like to get outside at night. A bit of patrolling. Keep an eye on things.

– That's comforting, East replies. – You've still got all your old gear, then?

– No, this is all surplus stuff. Pick it up cheap anywhere.

The peacocks go silent and the camp is enveloped by stillness, just the hum of the generators and rumble of the nearby Wash.

– I can't get cool.

– That's just the change of environment, nothing to worry about. You've been in the city too long.

– I thought it was colder by the sea.

– Not if you're not used to it. It can be very claustrophobic despite the open spaces.

East cannot get out of bed by daybreak. West lets him stay curled on the duvet and dresses for the day. He leaves with Conrad and fixes the door ajar.

Resigned to a day in the caravan, East is assaulted by visions and images. He hears laughing, tastes soot. Turns his face into the pillow. Sees West standing with his parents with arms entwined. Father with a skeletal face, still recognisable as Dad. Mother holding a photograph of him, waving it from side to side as if to a tune, an old pub tune, accompanied by a piano. Played by Keith. In combat strip.

Observing the sweat roll along his forearms and into his hands, then wiped on bed. Swigging water from the bottle kept on the shelf, feeling himself drown as he runs out of breath, the air bubbles rumbling to the base of the bottle like the last gasps of oxygen floating away. Fighting the tightening chest, ribs closing in on him, lungs struggling, his mouth burning.

After lunch West enters the caravan and flinches at his brother tied in knots. Burning alive with red skin aflame. Unable to douse himself with his sweat.

📖 I was going to the consultant. I wanted you to come. Discuss some of your concerns.

East can barely focus on the notepad. The book shudders in his fevered clutch. West waves his hands to disregard the idea, makes a grab for the pad.

📖 Another time?

He watches East shrink back on to the covers. Melting.

📖 Can I get anything?

East shakes his head, its movement restricted by contact with pillow.

– I can't take this.

West goes to leave, East calls him back.

– I'm sorry about the stuff yesterday.

West perches on the end of the bed. Takes out his pen.

📖 I understand what you were saying. It's just I've got all I want here. You've got to understand that.

– You obviously don't need me around.

Bitter words ejected like bile. West can think of nothing to say to appease his brother's agony, his sense of rejection.

East's day is lost in a daze. West returns late from Mary's and slips into the quilt with a check on his brother, curled up in a ball with hands and knees tucked under stomach. East is trying to sleep and cursing Keller's statement on the front planks. So much cooler in the shadows. Out of the heat, so much cooler. He uncurls himself at one a.m. and leaves the sleeping caravan to walk naked to the gate for the beach. Tempted by a plunge into ocean, a freezing immersion. Feeling as if he is dying under a coastal sky in the middle of night. Brother incapable of helping. Stepney incapable of helping. Metres from the breaking surf he collapses, before a lurking Keith can run to catch the body. Crying for help, Keith drags East along the sand back to camp, to the caravan, aided by Meredith and a waking West.

5

By morning East has stabilised, yet his mind still burns and his glands swell. West, Keith and Meredith sit by the bed. West holds East's arm while Meredith clutches West's hand. A chain of energy broken by Keith at the end who sips tea from polystyrene. A doctor and nurse arrive and usher the three guests out of the hospital room.

– I can't be left here, they'll get me! East shouts, raves over the nurse's shoulder, the doctor's head, the trolley laden with cartons, pills and rubber tubes.

– Relax, relax, you're okay, a nurse says, handing him medication. Her voice spreads over him, the pills float about his mouth in water, gulped cold, and soothes him into a haze.

East tries to shake Polly out of his head, as he swings left and then right. The stench of her unwashed body lying across him and a night at the grinding belt with Roger ahead of him. Suffocation, coughing and the hurling aside of hospital linen. Imagining Mary (looking like his grandmother) pulling West behind her, around her knees like a mother, a childhood West with a more defined head. Preventing East from contact with his brother.

– Can't catch me, can't catch me, West taunts, disappearing behind the skirt. East laughs and lunges at his brother, skipping around one side of Mary. West pops up behind the other leg. – Can't catch me.

East is brought back to the room by West stroking his hair and Keith standing tall at the foot of the bed, obscuring the wall clock.

– How are you feeling? Keith asks.

– Feel rough. Feel weird.

East assesses the room, the drawn curtains stroking the floor.

– I can't stay here, boys, East mumbles, still wrapped in fever.

– Don't worry. You'll be fine, assures Keith.

East attempts to shake off the terrible stiffness, the confusion.

– I'm serious, I can't stay here.

– We've got to go, they're not letting us stay here tonight. You'll be fine.

West gives a gentle punch on the arm, Keith winks, both head to the door.

– Keith, I'm serious, he says, climbing out of bed wearing a hospital smock, wavering on unbalanced legs, scanning the room for his clothes.

Keith stops and takes hold of East and pushes him back into bed.

– Do you really think these people are going to find you here?

– Yes.

6

Withered Arm has taken a phone call. The fifty pound note to the contact at the clinic is well spent. Tonight he can put to rest the threats from Garner, the taunts of comrades, his own self-doubts. The months spent in Norfolk on the only available trail of his quarry are to be rewarded. The blood of East will shower from the body like shaken champagne. Hit man will return to London with his reputation intact, perhaps enhanced, able to select easier jobs, bump up his prices. Succeeding for the Garners is worth three ordinary hits. And nothing would satisfy him more than watching the kid plead and squirm before thumping in two rounds and watching the expression transform from fear to horror to pain to death.

East sits awake with the television. Once again he is overcome by an urge to leave his bed and pull the handle to confirm it is locked. To turn the key and feel safe. The fourth time since midnight. It's now three a.m.

As he approaches the door, tiptoeing over the ammonia-wiped lino, there is a faint tap on the wood. East stands behind the locked entrance and awaits verification. Again the door taps and before he can assess the situation instinct erupts into question.

– Who is it?

There is no reply.

– Who is it? East repeats.

A sheet of paper from a notebook slides under the door.

📖 Guess?

West sits by the bed while East leans back on stacked pillows. East's head is clearer now that the medical staff have stifled the fever but he cannot repress the urge to give up the running and hurry back to Blackmore House and collapse into the bed left waiting for all these months. He looks at West, his brother who wants to stay in Norfolk, who wants to love an old woman, who no longer needs him. Sitting by the side of the bed as if he cares. As if nothing has changed.

📖 I thought I'd come back. I had to sneak out of the camp. Keith did not want to me to leave. Sorry it's so late.

– Cheers, East says, acting indifferent, letting the silence simmer between them.

West does not sense the tension and pushes back in the chair, incorporating a stretch into the movement.

East cannot hold back the boil.

– They've brainwashed you, that's what's happened, you know that?

West is surprised at the anger in his brother's voice. He looks up from the seat and stares at East's quivering face.

– They've wiped your mind, you know that?

West dispels the talk with a casual glance to the door. He has heard the envy routine before, at the Ranch, over Mary.

– Maybe that's what they want to do to me, get me to sit in some chair and suck out all my memories. You want to go back to the flat, I know you do, but you just can't remember that you do.

West is ready to repeat his well-worn lines of defence but is not prepared for a man in a black jacket with a stunted right arm to push open the door and stand in the corner with a handgun raised. The man who followed West through the empty corridors of the hospital and ducked into doorways while the brother inadvertently led the way to his target.

The man stands motionless with the weapon fixed on the patient. West automatically rises to his feet but East pushes him down with an outstretched hand.

East stares into the tunnel of the barrel. No light at the end. As there are no words. No messages from the Garners, nothing from the assassin's own repertoire of valedictions. No black humour to conclude the hunt. Just a victim and a gun.

Thump. Thump. Thump. Three rounds crash into the clinical quiet, crashing through cloth and into chest. A flash-flood of blood across the body, the head flopping back and then forwards, then sinking into death.

Another three bullets are pumped into the fallen frame, driven in by adrenalin, the ecstasy of victory. They splash the neck and skull.

East holds the Smith & Wesson in front of him, the

revolver is shuddering with panic. The weapon – a parting gift from Keith, slipped under the sheet – now hot and smoking.

The assassin wallows in a red lake. The man to be carried home in a box, to be paraded in front of those he sought to please. Planted in the ground and forgotten by those who paid for his services.

– It's what he would have wanted, the smirking cortège will mumble, hiding their grins from his grieving family.

The gunfire has aroused the hospital. East is pulling on clothes while West cannot pull his eyes from the corpse. The brothers leave bloody footprints along the corridor as they crash through doors, East hurls nurses and dazed patients to one side.

The weapon breaks through a car window and once again the two runaways find themselves strapping into an alien vehicle. East pumps the throttle, swallowing the car in a petrol fog, before spinning the wheels forward and aiming for the exit.

Leave-Taking

1

It is now four a.m. They are parked in a lay-by on the outskirts of Hunstanton. Sitting in silence, in darkness. West appears unmoved by the show of blood while East tries to accept the violence, stoked by fever and by the months of pressure, waiting for that moment when the past would catch up and emerge firing. All the time East has been running, the world about him has flattered to deceive; painting itself in the colours of the commonplace when nothing could ever be normal once Girl butted the stairs.

East plays tough, acts calm, but replays the six bullets over and over again as the assassin falls. He has fought with the gangs, lived on the estate, shared pints with killers from the vill who returned after bird, but never has he had to pull the trigger. Never has he had to execute.

A corner of moon squints from purple cloud. And now where to? East asks himself. No more escaping. It almost feels like time for a humane round into his own temple.

– If it's not here it's there, not there, here ... Fucking scum, running, gunning, who gives one, who fucking gives one? he mutters.

His mind sinks into dark images.

– Why have I got to live like this? Who poisoned my life?

Wet eyes loosen under the pain, under the strain of seeing only dark days ahead.

– Fuck this! What god is screwing my arse?

Final words before East throws his head on to the steering wheel, smashing the forehead on to the reinforced plastic. He pulls his head back against the headrest and slams the skull back on the wheel.

West grabs his brother around the head. – Norumf.

East eases into the embrace and waits for the anger to subside. Two minutes before he pulls himself free to breathe heavy and collect self-control. He places his hands on the car controls, checking the lights, the gears, the wheel.

📖 The ranch is not far.

– We're not going back to that dump.

West responds with a sudden turn of his head.

– That's right, we're going home. Where we should have gone a long time ago.

📖 The Garners?

– I'll deal with it.

📖 What about me? I want to go home to the camp.

– Oh no, West, I'm not letting you go back there where they fuck up your mind. I'm going to show you home, I'm going to show you what you're missing and what you seem to have forgotten.

East lets the engine tick over.

– Home, West, home. You and me, the old team. You'll soon remember all the good stuff, all the good times.

📖 I want to stay here. I f'ing told you!

– Whoa, calm down, calm it down. Trust me, I know what's good for you. Before East can close his insane smile, West is reaching for the handle. – Get off, West! Leave it!

East throws his arms over West as he tries to push the door open. – Frraffeet.

East flicks out punches with his left hand, the blows

becoming harder with each missed hit. But West does not stop, determined to get out. From his belt East reaches for the gun.

– Stop! he shouts, snatching the revolver and pushing the barrel into his brother's face. – Stop.

East pins West against the passenger window. The swollen flesh absorbs the metal.

– Now let's just drive in hush, yeah?

East's voice unrecognisable to West who closes his eyes and feels his sweat smudging and cooling against the glass. East puts the car in gear and turns on to the road. Both brothers pant, recovering from the struggle.

A cold wind blows in from the broken window. East clocks the signs for London and throws up a whoop.

2

The fever, the fears, the death all seem to dissipate as London approaches. East's enthusiasm is channelled through his leg on to the accelerator, pressing the car towards home.

His mind is full of plans. Full of memories. Ideas. He hums tunes he only half remembers, spits out of the window, continues to prod West with the gun, appears impervious to the danger that awaits him in Stepney. His desperation overwhelms reason, and as he drives he imagines securing mercy from the Garners. Begging leniency, offering money, service, whatever. Dropping in front of Father Garner and pleading for him to listen to the truth, to listen to innocence and call off the pack. Cowering for justice on an East End pavement, the soil of home kissed before the feet of Garner. Beseeching Bloke to embrace a Cockney brother who did no wrong, except run, and wants nothing more than to return home and live again. To forget lost months, to forget death, to exist in the security and certainty of Stepney. To prepare for another week of selling CDs and drinking profits. To laugh at Jerome, to get ready for the next party (and he remembers that he has missed Dawsey's), to lie in bed and smoke a cigarette thinking, Mmm, nice.

To forget Leafy, Noel, Bobby, Paddington, the Russian, Roger, Polly, Keith, the man with the withered arm and the gun.

To remember the flat, the boys, the boozer, Mum and Dad, West's models, making money, being cool.

To flick through memory: Girl naked, Jonesy laughing, Jocelyn serving, Berserkers, Jubilee Street, the dole office, Stepney Green station, Mile End Road, Karen Trimble, the branding on his bicep, the hum of the kitchen, the smell of warm pavement, the toilet seat, taxis to pubs stinking of aftershave and expectation, taxis from pubs stinking of Kronenberg and animosity, speed wraps, speed traps, baseball caps, bollards, lock-ups, Stepney accents (some fuckin' fing ly dat, yeh?), kebabs, winter coats, Boys Clubs, tattooed knuckles, forearms, necks, shoulders, earrings, chains, chokers, Saturday night poses, broken noses, wanks (handling swollen goods), dopiaza, the Irons, mobile phones, traffic cones, backhand loans, drum and bass, pool tables, dartboards, hangovers, handshakes, pills, swills, Vicky Park daffodils, Bombay Rolls, chippy, two-day pants, three-day socks, the wait for lift, the wait to sign on with numbered slip, next door's rows, upstairs' clumps, midnight humps, speed bumps, wire fences, dust, shaved heads, Bengali beats, Council Tax (You Are Now Entering Tower Hamlets), sweet wrappers, street rappers, bus stops with sloped bench, bedside lamp illuminating cupboard, Clement Atlee in frame, broken kerb, secondhand motors, thudding woofers, jazz funk, fighting talk, Rope Walk, stir-fried pork, wheelie bins, wrong numbers, stashing cash, techno, empty fridge, hanging up jackets, crisp packets, standing by twelfth-floor window thinking *jump*, ignoring the door buzzer, paying rent, talking shop, walking tall, forking out, cracking up, cracking down, breaking in, breaking out, taking on, making out, making off, pulling through, tuning the radio to hear 'big up' to Stepney and the Jubilee crew.

East's forehead is bruised and cut from where he thumped it against the steering wheel. His eyes are shining. He nods his head as he drives. He taps his fingers. He is ready to shoot his only brother if he prevents this homecoming.

3

Six a.m. East and West enter the flat at Blackmore House. Through the front door stained with soot and scrawl – *Die girl-killer*, *Scum*. The hallway is rotting with sprinkled water, burnt carpet and charcoal decor.

East is taking no chances with West, the gun is pressed firmly into his back to prevent an escape to the car and back to Norfolk, he pushes him along the trail of fire that stretches down the corridor. Into West's room, a cave of darkness despite the faint light eking into sky. Curtains frozen black, hanging like cadavers. The table reduced to a skeleton, balancing a model, now shrivelled crisp.

East ignores the cremation about him, looks through the destruction for clues to home. Pushes open the door to his own room and finds it untouched by flame. Shockingly bright and colourful next to the surrounding devastation. Not even smoke damage or heat marks or stains.

East takes West back into the living room, nothing but blackened shells left of the furniture and decorations. West makes a move for his notebook that East immediately notices, raising the gun in alarm. West squints, edges a nod towards the corner of the pad protruding from his pocket. East gives permission.

📖 We can't stay here. Come on, let's get out of here.

– Oh no, you don't get out of this that easily. I'm going to show you home.

📖 You're not well. You're not thinking straight.

– Is that what you think? Just what your arseholes would like you to think. You can't run away for ever.

West is about to write another note but East snatches away the book, hurling it to the other side of the room.

– I've read enough of your crap. It's my turn.

With a length of kite string West is tied up. His legs, body, arms and neck are bound around the steel limbs of an incinerated chair.

– This is for your own good, says East.

With West safely tethered East slips the gun back inside his belt and leaves the room. He returns minutes later with a few burnt models salvaged from West's room.

– See, remember the models. You loved models.

East flies the model plane with his hand, the aircraft barely recognisable without wings and propellers. Making engine and swooping noises, East flashes the decrepit plastic in front of West and pushes it through his hair. With spare string East fastens the three models (plane, boat and space rocket) to the light-fitting dangling over the chair. West sits among the decorations, pushing each model aside with his head only to have them swing back and hit him in the face.

– Playing with them already. I knew you'd be glad to see them.

East goes to his room and rifles through the rails of clothing. He finds the Berserker jacket and brings it to West.

– You always wanted one of these, didn't you, Westy?

Carefully the jacket is draped over the prisoner's shoulders and left to hang precariously.

– Happy? East says, smiling a tortured grin.

West shakes his head, looking to the floor to avoid the tragedy of his brother's grief. His brother's humiliation.

– Saveloy and chips, that's it. How you loved saveloy and chips, East suddenly recalls, forgetting the years of closed mouth and blended meals.

– How about I pop out for a takeaway?

West does not take his eyes off the floor, the blackened floor.

– Yeah, that'll cheer you up. Back in a tick.

The moment East is out of the door West wrestles with the knots and binding, tensing muscles and relaxing, jerking hands, throwing himself forward hoping to loosen his captivity. But the string is strong, wrapped around in quantity. As he struggles to escape, the models continue to bounce against his head.

East saunters along Stepney Way oblivious to the early morning hour, the slow-moving cars and chilled air. He waves at the occasional pedestrian on the other side of the road, their tired eyes return a reluctant stare and upwards nod. Finding the chip shop closed he swaggers into the adjoining newsagent.

– Do you sell chips? he asks the man behind the counter.

– No, sir, comes the reply. – But we do sell potato crisps, he adds.

– What about saveloy? Sell saveloy?

The rest of the day is spent with West tied to the chair and East playing through his extensive music collection.

– Oh yeah, how about this one, he shouts, over the volume.

– This is music! he cries, dancing about the room.

And then there are long periods of silence when East just lies on the floor, puffing on a cigarette and watching the ash fall on to his chest.

By evening East is preparing to visit the Black Horse. Plucking out various items of clothing and throwing them on to the bed in his room. The months on the run have thinned him, and each shirt and pair of trousers droop from his body. Every combination is paraded in front of West who is forced to watch his brother prance about wearing oversized clothes and a psychotic gaze.

– Not sure about the green with the grey, are you?

– These shoes are too clumpy.

– Remember this old number, Westy?

– This jumper's bloody well grown.

Finally deciding on his outfit East stands in front of West, his arms crossed and legs standing apart, looking down on his captive. East does not see the strain on his brother's face, the red neck. All he can offer are quick words of departure.

– I'm off to the swiller. I'm going to sort out the Garners, get us sorted to stay. How about that, bro?

– Prrummpum (Just go).

It is early evening, the first few punters are in the pub drinking in the after-work silence. Duke is behind the bar;

Dawsey, Jonesy, Tops are on stools. The four of them watch East walk to the bar in his shaggy clothes, his shoulders dipping and rolling with each step.

– Evening all, he says.

– East? queries Tops.

– What you on, Topsy? A big K? I'll get 'em in.

The four are shut in silence at the appearance of a comrade given up for dead. The entrance of a face that is not meant to be there.

– What sort of welcome is this?

Still no one can muster a response.

– You've got to get the fuck out of here, Tops manages to mumble. – I'm not going to end up like Dartford.

The warning thaws the confusion and Duke is on his way from behind the bar.

– What do you mean, like Dartford?

– What do you think I fucking mean? He went down for you.

Before East can respond, Duke is in his face.

– Uh-uh, he says. – I'm not having you in here. I'm not having this, not tonight. He puts an arm around East and gently prises him away from the bar. – Sorry, East, but I can't have this going on.

– But I've sorted it with the Garners, I've sorted it.

– When? Duke asks.

Hesitation. Deceit exposed.

– Clear out, East, Dawsey adds, to the pull of Duke's arm. – We won't say nothing.

– Fuck you, wankers. Fuck you! This is my home too.

– Not until we're told it is, says Duke, his force now showing in breathless words and veined arms.

Anger is shelved and East tries another tack.

– Please, guys. You're my friends, I need you.

He's dismissed with streetwise nonchalance.

– Bye, the three seated drinkers say in unison.

East goes straight to his room without a word for West. He lies on the bed, face into pillow, hands tucked underneath his chest. The muted thud of music playing downstairs, the rich scent of scorched wood seeping under the door. The bed does not feel right, it is not comfortable. The duvet is starchy, musty, entangled in his flattened hands. He looks up, raising his shoulders and pressing down his lower back, and notices a slip of colour on the bedside table. It is a picture of him and West taken on their last night at home. In the pub, snapped by Jonesy with a camera snatched off Willsy.

A flick of the switch and the lamp shines. East takes the photograph and turns on to his front. Analyses the print, so much brighter than he recalls, flash giving shine to features and pint glasses pushed into frame. A rare picture because West is so loath to pose for the camera. But this time West is coerced by his dominant brother with an arm clenched about his neck. His resentment exposed by the hollow glare. The expression shows a pain that East had not seen before. A pain etched over swollen skin and ingrained in the lines of every facial contour. Unlike East, trapping his brother with hilarity and laughing with drunken, amphetamine recklessness, not noticing the head to which he clings.

East is hypnotised by the photograph, it takes him away from the madness and confusion of his homecoming. Gradually, a semblance of order returns to an exhausted, stretched mind.

East rolls over to sit on the edge of the bed, staring at the tortuous glare of the brother he thought he had loved so well. Why didn't he tell me? East thinks. Why didn't he shout at me? Forced into the picture, forced into a life that he did not want. Forced back to London and tied to a chair. With that image East springs from the bed and into the living room to his hostage. Confronted by an empty chair with lines of string draped at its feet. West has gone.

East goes to the window and looks out on evening grey, to the car park hazy under streetlight. The car has also gone.

On the chair is a page from West's notebook. East grabs the message. He does not recognise the scrawl – it is not West's – not until he reads the threat. The hand of Garner.

▤ Open the door. It's time to go.

Complicit neighbours heard the voices through the walls, whispered behind locked doors on the twelfth, nodded knowingly at East's voice, phoned through the news and now wait in adjoining hallways to hear the Girl-killer scream.

They have already heard the wails of West as he begged mercy for East after the Garners untied him. After the Garners picked the front-door lock and found West strapped to burnt chair. They sent him running. To the car, to the Black Horse, to miss East by minutes. To be apprehended by Cousin Garner at the ground-floor lifts and told to clear out while Geezer and Bloke knock on the door. West fought, grunted, spat, clawed, but Cousin was too powerful.

– You're too late.

– Ffummraannt.

– Don't make it harder for yourself, boy.

– Ummamman.

East hears the door. Hears a Garner voice.

– Open up, East. Time to go.

This was the moment East had anticipated. The moment to hit the floor and adore the feet of Geezer. But there is not time, they are coming through the door. Geezer and Bloke stand gargantuan in the hall, in dusty light. There is not time for protestations of innocence or knee-scrabbling pleading, the two giants are walking towards him with hammer and machete. East makes a grab for the revolver stashed in his pants, his eyes wild as the weapon flounders in his unstable grip. Click. Click. Click. Empty chambers. Only six rounds. Deposited earlier. There is no time for respite. East shrinks to the floor, the gun slipping from his hands, his mouth breaking open to howl silence. A mouth shaped to scream a mute goodbye to Stepney.

4

A baby lies in a cot. It cries for food. A mother scrambles out of bed to take the little girl; a new child, an adopted child. Taken from the East End to the suburbs. To be given a start in life. The mother holds her baby in front of the open curtains and looks out on the sleeping houses, wrapped in trees and bushes. A world of comfort. And opportunity.

5

West's hands shake as he grips the steering wheel. His head is full of shapes and sounds and shouts. Unable to remember East as he was. Only in his desperation. His confusion. Madness. Unable to remember Stepney as it was. Only as a bad smell. Foul taste. Sadness.

The tower block will remain; standing decrepit like a giant old man. And the shadows will remain. And the broken swings. And the headstones in Mile End. But the noise of memory and mourning fades as West drives further away from London and nearer to Norfolk. To Hunstanton; where Mary waits. To the Holme caravan; where Conrad's sleeping breath blends with the sound of the rolling tide.